BR⋯⋯
EYES

FRANCES IVE

five press

Brown Eyes
Copyright © 2021 by Frances Ive.

Typesetting: Inksnatcher
Cover design: German Creative

ISBN   978-1-7399768-0-4

In memory of Benji

FOREWORD

Animals are sensitive creatures and pick up on the mood of the people they live with. It struck me when we had a Labrador how affected he was by what was going on around him. If there was an argument he hid under the table, if any of us was upset he looked unhappy, but of course when we were joyful, he loved it.

That's when I had the idea about a dog watching everyone in the family and seeing what was going on. This fictional story is written from two viewpoints, those of both Meriel, the main woman, and Benji the Labrador. It is not my story, but he was my dog.

1

Like a fly on the wall. From the inside out. The heart of the family. The only one to see it all.

Benji

My perfect life is under threat. I have always thought my life was very good and that I lived with the best family in the world. I don't know a lot about people, but I am very well treated and everyone in the family loves me. Obviously, I love them too and I would do anything for them, but life has completely changed.

Something happened last night and I don't really understand what it was, but I know that something is very wrong. There was a terrible row last night and Meriel was horrible to Phil, but I think he might have deserved it.

I think there is a huge problem. I am a very sensitive creature, and I can hear it in

Brown Eyes

their voices, see it in their faces and feel it in my body. I'd just drifted off to sleep and I could hear that ring ring noise but no one was answering it. Then I heard Meriel in the next room saying,

'Who's there? Who's there?'

I sat up. Meriel sounded desperate and then she threw that thing she speaks into on the floor and collapsed on to the sofa. I leapt out of my bed, jumped over the pile of papers on the floor and moved up close to her. She was crying and there were wet tears all over the place, which I tried to lick. They were very salty. I put my paw on her and cried too. What had happened – was she ill?

She touched me to reassure me but still she carried on with this crying and a kind of low moaning like an animal in pain. I think I fell asleep again, because when I woke up it was quite cold and she was lying on the sofa still. I was curled up right next to her.

I could hear his car and he walked in furtively and switched on the hall light. He took his coat off and quietly removed his shoes. I started to bark and he whispered loudly,

'Be quiet. It's only me.'

I was so pleased to see him that I rushed up to him as he opened the kitchen door. My tail was wagging so hard that I was banging the fridge door loudly.

Brown Eyes

Meriel was awake by then but was still slouched on the sofa. Phil walked into the lounge towards the sofa as if he didn't know she was there. Of course, he can't smell her like I can. He clicked on the light.

'Meriel. What are you doing?'

He looked at the empty bottle and looked towards her. Her face looked really red.

'What's the matter love? Why are you up?'

I sensed a very strong atmosphere that I didn't altogether like. There was so much tension in the air that I could feel it in my skin, and I didn't want to be there. My tail dropped between my legs and I looked from one to the other.

'Had a good time I suppose?' she said in a slurred voice that's nothing like her.

'No, just routine you know. Just arguing with these contractors down at Plymouth.'

'Really? Did they feel good? Did they?'

'What do you mean?'

'You know what I mean, you lying bastard. You know what I mean.' She sat up and slumped forward.

'You've been in bed with someone else. I know it.'

'Don't be so ridiculous. You've had too much to drink.'

'And you think having too much to drink makes me incapable of knowing the sound of my filthy husband's voice when he's shagging

Brown Eyes

someone? Who was it? That tart in the office? That one who's always got different blokes. Are you one of them? Are you in a long line, or does she love you? That bitch?'

'What are you talking about?'

'Philip, I know what you've been doing. Will you stop denying it?'

'Denying what?'

She picked her speaking thing up from the floor and hurled it at him and it hit him hard on the arm. His face contorted – maybe he thought that she was mad.

'You rang me, you rang me, and I heard it all. What are you some kind of sadist? You wanted me to hear you.'

Phil's face changed as if he had just seen a ghost.

'I can explain.'

'How do you explain infidelity? You can explain it in court.'

'Now come on Meriel. Be reasonable. You haven't wanted me for ages. What is a man supposed to do?'

'Oh, so that's it now. It's my fault, is it? Very clever, of course everything always has to be my fault, doesn't it? It takes two you know Phil. I'm not putting up with it for a moment longer.'

'What do you mean by that?'

'I want a divorce.'

'What? For an infidelity – one?'

Brown Eyes

'One what? One time, or one woman? I don't believe a word you say. You've probably been doing this for years.'

I couldn't stand this anymore so I turned round and walked slowly out of the room. This was not going to improve and I can't bear hearing them tear each other apart.

'I'll talk to you when you're sober Meriel. This is ridiculous. We have to resolve it for the sake of the kids.'

'You should have thought of that before. I'm not resolving anything. It's too late.'

She almost fell off the sofa, pulled herself up and staggered upstairs. Phil came over and sat by my bed. I was a bit torn, because I knew he'd upset her, but he is my master, so I tried to look neutral. It was hard for me to believe that he could do something awful, but surely, they couldn't be apart. Who would get custody of me?

He stroked my head and said,

'I've been a complete fool. I don't know what made me do it, but you know Benji perhaps I'm weak. I just couldn't resist it when she came on strong but I don't want to lose everyone, even you.'

I tried to let him know through my eyes that I felt overwhelmed with love and sorrow.

In my normal life, which happened before this, I can be happy every day provided I get a walk. It doesn't matter whether it's raining, snowing or horribly windy I still love it

Brown Eyes

because the open air is full of smells and sounds that make it so exciting. I especially love the beach and being able to run in the water and out again and meeting other dogs there and swimming.

The countryside is full of other interesting animals that I sometimes watch, and, I have to admit, I sometimes chase. Birds are everywhere but the other day I saw one that walked really slowly and had lots of pretty coloured feathers. I often chase foxes because I don't like them, but they always get away. I wonder what I would do if I ever caught one.

I used to be able to get up to a rabbit and once I picked one up, but my mouth is very soft, so I didn't hurt it and Meriel made me put it down. So now I just look at them and watch to see if they're going to run away or not. They remind me of cats and I don't want to get scratched.

For some reason all of the Stevensons get very cross when I run off to see other dogs. I just can't control myself because I smell them and see them and I all I want is to play with them and sniff them. Even though I hear them shouting at me, something in me ignores them because I want to play so much.

We've got a cat at home and I can tolerate it but it's not very keen on me. The house we live in has a nice straight lawn where I lie in summer and at the end of the lawn are a few trees that give me plenty of shade on hot days.

Brown Eyes

In the summer the house has lots of red and pink flowers growing around the front door, and I love the smells.

It's a quiet street with lots of people who all seem very friendly and at the back is this wonderful park that leads into a football field and then some woods. I just love it there.

2

Meriel

I've never felt like this before. I suppose I've prided myself on being a good listener and spending many an hour going over and over my friends' problems. People have such complicated lives, and I have been guilty in the past of feeling a bit smug that mine was so good, so simple.

What a mistake. It obviously wasn't as good as I thought it was. I must have kidded myself and overlooked our lack of affection, lack of touching, and that we don't ever talk to each other properly about anything that isn't mundane routine stuff, usually about the kids. It's so easy to carry on a life thinking it's all fine, but when do Phil and I ever spend time together? I think we've forgotten who we are. I can barely remember that guy I fell in love with – it's so long ago, that it feels like another lifetime.

Of course, some of this seems normal because so many of our friends are in the same boat. Some of my girlfriends plan to leave their husbands or partners when the children are eighteen and I wonder if they

Brown Eyes

will. It has always struck me as extremely sad, but now out of the blue I'm in this situation.

I noticed my cup of coffee and it had gone cold. I had to start work again soon. I said I'd do this project at home but I'm not doing anything but mooning around feeling miserable. If it weren't for the fact that I have always given the impression that we are love's young dream it might be a bit easier. How do you tell people that you and your husband who are so 'happily married' are splitting up, that he's run off with some young girl?

I realised that the phone was ringing. I didn't feel like talking to anyone.

'Hello.'

'What's wrong?' Tania asked. She knew me so well.

'Nothing. I just don't feel well, that's all. I've taken time off work because of my stomach.'

My voice didn't sound like mine, and now I was even lying to my best friend.

'You sound really miserable. Everything else is all right then?'

'Yes, of course it's fine.'

Why was I doing this? Why couldn't I tell my friend? I'm so Mrs. Perfect that I just could not admit it.

'Do you want to come over for lunch next Friday? You don't work on Fridays, do you?'

Brown Eyes

'No,' I couldn't think of an excuse quickly enough.

'That's fine. Thanks.'

Benji

I love it when we go round to Tania's house because Meriel always takes me, and their retriever is really good fun. It was one of those early spring days which are cold at night but warm enough for them to sit on the patio sipping cups of tea and chatting. I caught some of the conversation when I wasn't running round with Tanzy.

Meriel didn't look like she normally does. She had nice clothes on but under her eyes was all black and there were little lines all over her face that weren't normally there. She kept opening and shutting her mouth like a dog trying to catch a fly, and puffing and blowing as if she was running.

Tania looked much slimmer and had a very tight top on again that accentuated her breasts, and her jogging pants didn't come down to her feet and looked very tight. Tania used to be quite a large lady, but she was now top heavy with huge breasts and a slim bottom! I think human men like that.

'Once again you look pretty good Tania. This trainer chap must be good for you,' Meriel remarked.

Brown Eyes

Tania laughed like a puppy.

'He is.'

'So, is he good looking?' Cathy asked.

'He's gorgeous,' Tania said. She looked like Elly, Meriel's daughter, when she's talking about some pop star.

'Is there something you want to tell us?' Meriel asked.

'What do you mean?' She was taunting them. There must be something to tell.

'You seem very vibrant.'

'It does me good. He does me good. In fact, I just love being with him.'

'Doing running and playing tennis?' Meriel said, but she looked as if she might laugh, which was of course an improvement to how she's been lately, in some kind of hell.

'Yes of course. That as well.'

'As well?' Cathy almost shrieked.

'As well as what?' Tania sniggered. She was enjoying this.

'Just enjoying his company.'

'Is he available?' Meriel asked.

'Well yes and no.'

'What do you mean?' Cathy intervened. She kept smiling too.

'He is single if that's what you mean.'

'Yes, but does he have anyone permanent?'

'No. Why are you asking?' Tania smiled, in a knowing sort of way.

Brown Eyes

'I think I'm getting a very strong impression that something's going on between you and Paul,' Meriel laughed.

'He's half my age. Don't be ridiculous.' Again, the silly laugh.

'How old is he then?'

'Thirty-two on 7th June.'

'And, you even know his birthday?' Cathy almost screamed.

'What else do you think we talk about when we're jogging across the moors?'

'Yes. I suppose you have plenty of time to talk, don't you?' Cathy said.

'We do. And sometimes we go for lunch as well.'

'Gosh that sounds awfully friendly,' Meriel said, looking quite jealous.

'Look. I must admit I fancy this guy like crazy but he's very young.'

As Tania said this, she stuck her chest out. I don't know if that was significant.

'Well, you're only forty-seven, Tania,' Cathy said.

'But you're married,' Meriel adds.

'Small detail. If you can call it being married with someone like Dave.'

'What do you mean?' Meriel's face looked all serious again. I didn't want her to be upset. She continued, 'I've always thought of you as a really good couple. You have always given that impression.'

Brown Eyes

'Oh, come on. I must be a good actress. I have put up with Dave for all these years so maybe I had to justify it to myself. But quite honestly, I don't see us as having a good marriage. He goes his own way and now I'd like to go mine.'

Meriel was going all red in the face. I shifted myself around so I could be close to her.

'Are you going to do something about it, Tania?'

'I doubt it. I don't do things like that do I?'

'You never know,' Cathy said.

Meriel looked at Cathy, who said,

'What's up Meriel? You look a bit upset.'

'I am really. I can't believe that you would just go and cheat on Dave. After all these years. He really loves you.' She sounded really cross.

'Does he hell? Whatever makes you think that? I am very convenient because I sort his life out for him, but I am just like a mother to him. He never for one minute makes me feel as if he cares about me. And going out on a Friday and coming back on Sunday without telephoning isn't really what you expect someone who cares about you to do is it?'

'I never knew it was that bad,' Meriel mumbled.

Cathy nodded,

Brown Eyes

'Quite honestly Tania, I think if you can have a bit of fun with this guy just go for it.'

Meriel's mouth dropped open, like a dog's.

Cathy got up and hugged Tania. 'You deserve it, you really do.'

'Thanks Tania.'

She obviously knew more about Tania's marriage than Meriel did, and I could see Meriel wasn't happy about this. She was staring at the floor. I hope they knew what to say to her. They were my only hope.

Cathy, who is a lovely sensitive lady, put her hand on Meriel.

'You're not alright, are you? What's the matter?'

'Surely it hasn't upset you that much Merry, what I've said?' Tania asked, a bit harshly, I thought.

'It's not you. I am jealous in a way and I'm really a bit upset about infidelity because of well, I must tell you about Phil.'

They stare at her.

'He's having an affair, and he's leaving.'

'Oh no Meriel. What happened?'

'I heard him on my mobile phone. It rang by mistake while he was, he was, you know, sh…having it off with her.'

'Who, who is she?'

'Laura, Laura from the office.'

'You know her?'

Brown Eyes

'I've seen her, spoken to her, I know who she is. She's young and drop-dead gorgeous. Not old and frumpy like me.'

They both shook their heads but didn't say anything.

Meriel carried on,

'You know how young girls have such lovely skin. We must have all had it once upon a time, but now I really notice it. It just makes me feel awful thinking of him touching her, and thinking how perfect she is, and how flawed I am.'

Tania was a big mother earth lady. Now she was a thinner mother earth lady and she put her arms round Meriel. I started whining because I was sort of jealous, but I was also upset and worried too and I wanted Tania to help her.

'You poor love.'

Meriel burst into tears.

'Come on,' Tania said. 'It's good to cry – let it all out.'

I didn't think so because I just cannot bear it. I made even louder crying noises as well – they were just coming out of me naturally, because of how I was feeling. Cathy glanced at me, but all her attention was on their friend.

'I've told him I want a divorce and he's going to move out.'

'Just like that?'

Brown Eyes

'Well yes. Just like that. What else can I do?'

'Try and patch it up?' Tania suggested.

'What with a bloody adulterer? It wasn't as if it was great before but the insult, the insult of it all.'

'Your pride is hurt,' Tania continued.

Suddenly it all went silent, and they seemed to all look at nothing, which was unnerving to say the least. I'd rather they talked or shouted than this. So, when Tanzy nudged me to go down the garden I was only too pleased for an excuse to get away. I loved this garden. There were different parts to it. The patio, where the girls sit and discuss their marriages, and the big lawn with a wood at the end of it. There are lots of smells and animals in there. When I got back Meriel seemed to be talking in sobs, like children often do.

'Just explain it to me slowly, in your own time,' Tania said in a soothing voice that almost made me feel better too. It's as if she was in charge and was going to make it all right. I lay down and pretended to sun myself, but really I wanted to hear what actually happened on that fateful night, because I don't really know. I only saw my side of it.

'He said he was working, he's always saying it, and last Friday the phone rang, and it was late. I was watching a film and

Brown Eyes

drinking, drinking. I could hear them – you know what I mean.'

I didn't know what she meant, but they both wobbled their heads up and down like nodding dogs.

'His mobile, it was in his pocket, and he'd rung me without knowing, and I couldn't believe it as he was saying, "Come here," and then I could hear the sound of...'

She started snuffling and shoved a tissue under her nose. Tania took her back in her arms.

'I'll get you a drink and you can tell us about it.'

For some reason humans seem to think that having a drink makes them able to talk, and it is only a cup of tea, not that strong stuff in a bottle.

They discussed it over and over so many times that I knew the story backwards. What he did, what he said, what Laura (the other woman, I think) might have said, why he did it, what she shouldn't do, what she could do.

'Look Meriel, do you have to split up? One infidelity isn't enough to break up with someone is it?'

Splitting up – this was serious. Who would have me?

'You sound like my mother,' Meriel said, rather ungraciously I thought. I, for one, knew

Brown Eyes

what her mother is like and that was definitely an insult.

'But you love him don't you,' Tania insisted. 'If it's just a fling, is it worth splitting up the family?'

That word again – I was terrified.

'I can't, I just can't. I don't trust him, and I did love him but how can he love me to do something like this? Why should I do all the loving, the forgiving and have him back when all he'll do is do it again?'

A large tear rolled down her face and I just couldn't resist going up and nuzzling her. I wanted to lick it, but I couldn't reach her head as she was sitting upright.

'How sweet,' Tania said. 'They know, you know. You don't know that he will do it again, but maybe it was because things weren't right between you. These problems are usually 50-50, aren't they? You've felt unhappy about certain things and maybe you're not communicating.'

'Like you and Dave you mean.'

'What do you mean?'

'Well, the way you're carrying on with that trainer – he's young enough to be your son.'

Cathy put her hand on Meriel as if to shut her up. Why was she being horrible to her best friend now? She was hard to understand sometimes, even though I do love her.

Brown Eyes

'I'm sorry Tan, that was uncalled for – I don't feel good and I don't want to be horrible to you. I spend enough of my life being horrible to the kids and to Phil as well.'

Oh no, she looked like she was going to cry again. We'd been in this garden with them talking about whether Cathy was going to die or not, and now we were here going over my owners' marriage. It was all too much. I just wanted an easy untroubled life.

Tania was looking at her right in the eyes.

'You need to sort this out Merry. There are two of you here who love each other from all I can see and because he's done something stupid you can't work it out and stay together. What does he want to do?'

'Well of course he doesn't want to go because he would probably like to have his cake and eat it. But I'm not putting up with it, I can tell you. He can't do this to me and get away with it.'

I pricked up my ears at the thought of cake, but no one looked very cheerful so I must have got it wrong.

'I can understand you feeling angry,' Cathy said.

'Can you, can you really? When you've got a doting husband like Andy.'

'Well, he may appear to be that way, but he isn't really.'

Brown Eyes

'He wouldn't ever behave like that though, would he?'

'I suppose not but how do we know? They say 70 percent of men are unfaithful.'

'I'm sure Dave has been unfaithful,' Tania said. 'Half the time he gets so drunk he won't even know where he's been the night before so if he ended up in bed with someone so much the better. But I don't care anymore.'

'That's how I want to be. I just don't want to care.'

'What about the children?'

'It's obviously not going to be easy, but they can carry on seeing Phil.'

Cathy leant forward, 'Are you sure you want this Meriel?'

'No. I didn't want him to screw this Laura or whatever her stupid name is, but I can't let him walk all over me, can I? He can't get away with it.'

'But you will be hurt as well Meriel – it's not just punishing Phil.'

'I know but punishing Phil might give me satisfaction.'

'Do you really think so?'

'Yes, I do.'

'I think you should think very carefully about this Meriel,' Tania said.

'Like you and, no forget it. Sorry. I can't compare it. Sorry Tania.'

She started crying again.

Brown Eyes

'You're upset so I'm not going to take it seriously. But it might surprise you to know that I made up my mind fifteen years ago to leave Dave.'

'What?' Meriel looked shocked.

'When he missed the third birth in a row, I decided I'd had enough.'

'How have you got through the last fifteen years?'

'By knowing that I'd go when I could. And when I have an opportunity, I'm not going to turn it down.'

'What with this trainer?' Meriel sounded disapproving. 'Look, I'm sorry. Your life isn't the same as mine. It's just infidelity that's my weak spot at present.'

'I know. And I also know you love Phil. So why hurt yourself?'

'I've made up my mind and he's moving out next week.'

Cathy and Tania looked at each other. I closed my eyes and wished I could close my ears. Sometimes Meriel was so stubborn.

3

Benji

'I hate my parents, both of them, they make my life miserable. But you, you're different. You're my only friend. We could run away together, let's do it tonight. We'll go after dinner when they're busy arguing with each other and we'll go and stay in that deserted farmhouse, and we'll eat blackberries and potatoes. Isn't that a good idea?'

Ricky was lying on his bed playing on that play station thing again while he told me what he wanted to do with his life, and mine. I think I'm the only one he ever talks to like this, and I do love him so, but I love them all. I'm so scared that something's going terribly wrong with my family.

'Ricky, get up,' his mother's voice thundered up the stairs. She stormed through his door and looked at the floor, the bed and the cupboards, all covered in clothes, sports gear, schoolbooks and paraphernalia.

'It's time you tidied up this mess and what is Benji doing in here with you? Come on, you're getting really lazy these days.'

Brown Eyes

Meriel was in a bad mood again. What had happened to the lovely woman she used to be, who had time for her kids and who was kind to everyone? I must say I'm lucky because she still reserves her kindness for me, but she's so horrible to Elly and Ricky these days that I feel sorry for them. And what has he done wrong? Surely, he's entitled to a rest.

'I keep telling you to tidy up this room and you never do. I'm going to cut down on your pocket money if you don't do it now. I've had enough.'

With that she stormed out of the room and Ricky gently stroked my head.

'See what I have to put up with Benji. She's an old bag.'

I could hear Meriel in the next room having a go at Elly.

'These trousers have been lying on the floor for two weeks and now you tell me you want them tomorrow.'

Unlike her brother Elly didn't take it lying down.

'Leave me alone, get out of here, I hate you.'

'Don't you dare speak to me like that you, you …'

Ricky got up and shut the door and started playing his horrible music loudly. Meriel came to the door and banged hard on the door.

Brown Eyes

'Turn that racket down – do you want to make the neighbours deaf?'

Ricky must be deaf already because he didn't move an inch and Meriel burst into the room again.

'How many times have I got to tell you – turn it down?' She walked over to the computer and turned it down so even I could hardly hear it. I was slowly trying to sneak under the bed, but there was so much stuff under it that I couldn't squeeze in. I was halfway under with my bottom sticking out.

'Come on Benji, now.'

I slowly followed. I want to stay in everyone's good books. She stomped down the stairs and I went down two paws at a time.

When we got down to the kitchen she sat at the table with her head in her hands.

'What's the matter with me Benji? I keep shouting at them all. I've got so much else going wrong in my life that I keep taking it out on them.'

She started crying. I'd seen this too often lately and I can't bear it. I nuzzled up to her and put my head on her lap hoping she'd stop if I was nice to her. Instead, she took my head in her hands and leant forward and cried on my head. I could feel wet tears dripping on my fur like rain, and I wanted to cry too but I knew she needed my support, so I held on to my feelings.

Brown Eyes

This was the happiest household in the world when I came here as a puppy, and I had always felt that I was a blessed animal. Everyone was gentle and nice to me and they always used to laugh, but that was before things went wrong. Now I only hear Elly laugh when she's with her friends and then they giggle a lot, but not when the family is all together.

Meriel tore off some kitchen roll and wiped my fur.

'I'm so glad I've got you because you just sit and listen and you're not there to pass judgement on me, and I'm sure you care.'

I wished I could speak and shout, 'I do, I do, I do, and I can't stand seeing this family falling apart'.

And if only I could do something about it, sit and talk to them, make them see sense, make her understand that this other woman just didn't matter. It's like me running off with my friends – I always wanted to come back to my own family.

There was a ring and she got up and sounded all happy speaking to the machine. I couldn't do that, just switch on a new mood. I was so fed up I thought I'd go to sleep and maybe it would all go away.

I went back to my basket and closed my eyes. It was getting so exhausting all this emotion. The next thing I knew I could hear Phil bellowing.

Brown Eyes

'It didn't mean anything. When are you going to get that into your stupid head?'

'If it didn't mean anything, why did you do it? Why did you decide to ruin our lives?'

'No, Meriel you decided to ruin our lives. You're the one who won't give it another go. I'd do anything to try and patch it up.'

'What? Even stop seeing HER!' she shouted her eyes filled with tears. 'Would you do that?'

'I have stopped seeing her. I just want to be with you and the kids.'

The door opened and in walked Elly. She honestly pretended that nothing unusual was happening, or maybe she was deaf too.

'What's the matter with Benji? He looks really depressed.'

Well, I am, and I'm amazed you aren't as well. She comes over to me and starts kissing my head and cuddling me. I must look depressed more often.

'Elly, hurry up. Don't forget we've got Guides later and you won't have done that work you had to do for tomorrow will you?'

Elly ignored her mother. Phil put his arm round his daughter and she gave him a big hug.

'Look Dad, Benji looks really depressed. Do you think dogs have things they worry about?'

Brown Eyes

'Not really darling. They haven't got brains like we have so they just worry about things that are instinct like where's the next meal and isn't it time for a walk?'

He laughed. I didn't think that was very funny. Meriel was banging cupboards really loudly as if she didn't like it either.

'Get ready, Elly. Phil, have you rung that man about the insurance yet? And by the way.'

She watched Elly leaving the room, and when she'd gone, she said the worst words I have ever heard.

'I'm keeping Benji.'

'He's my dog,' Phil retorted.

'He was your dog. He comes with the family and besides the children love him.'

'But I chose him and wanted him, you didn't even want him,' Phil insisted.

'That was five years ago now and he's a part of our lives. You're not around to feed him and walk him, are you? So, there's no choice.'

'We could have joint custody,' he smiled.

'It's not debatable and it isn't funny,' she said, and the tears started back in her eyes. I can't stand it.

She banged down a glass and it broke, shattering pieces everywhere on the floor.

'Now look what you made me do,' Meriel screamed at Phil.

Brown Eyes

'I suppose it's my fault, is it?'

Phil grabbed my red lead and I jumped up.

'Come on Benji, let's go for a walk.'

You couldn't see me for dust. I wanted out of this dreadful atmosphere and a walk in the park into the bargain.

I was on the lead as we walked down the road to the park and there was no one else around.

'You have an easy life, Benji,' Phil said patting me on the head.

I turned my head to look him directly in the eyes to make him realise that I knew what he was saying, but I completely disagreed. I don't call this life, as it is currently, easy at all.

'Yes, you do. None of this hassle with women. I made one mistake and it didn't mean anything and now I am going to lose everything. I can't bear it.'

I thought he was going to cry. I'd never seen that before and I really didn't want to. I stopped and looked sympathetic again.

'You're so faithful and loyal and I'm going to lose you as well as my children and wife. Perhaps I could use you as a bargaining tool, insist that I have you and that Meriel has the children and then she'll give in. What do you think?'

I didn't like the sound of it at all. I don't think I want to be doggy in the middle of this mess with them fighting over me, but he was

Brown Eyes

upset so I stood right by his leg leaning on him to show solidarity. I love them all so I don't take sides. All I want is for them to stay together forever so that nothing changes.

4

Meriel

There was barely time to think as the children need to be ferried all over the place. I felt so miserable and wondered at how the children didn't seem to notice although Ricky peered at me once or twice. They were so obviously in their own little worlds that they didn't pick up on my state of mind.

I felt like starting to smoke again and on top of all my problems Phil and I had to go to a party at Tania's. It was Dave's fiftieth and we couldn't get out of it. At least Phil was off playing golf (as if life were completely normal) so at least I wouldn't have to face him during the day.

I needed to take Ricky to football and pick him up before getting Elly over to her friends to go ice skating. And I'd offered to take three other girls so I had to do it. Listening to them chatting away was quite therapeutic because they were so excited about everything. I couldn't imagine being like that anymore.

I've known for a long time that our relationship was not good. Half of my friends are separated or divorced, and I wondered

Brown Eyes

why we'd carried on, but now I supposed we would become a statistic too.

It was going through my head the whole time what Mum would say. My bloody mother. I do love her obviously, but she is so hard to talk to. It would be my fault, as it always is in her eyes.

I looked at my black dress and thought of Mum saying, 'Going to a funeral?' Well yes, I was actually – my own. I rejected the black dress. I put on some heavy eye make-up and chose a slinky aubergine (isn't that what they called it?) coloured velvet dress that was very low cut. For some reason I was making extra special effort to look good, but who for? Maybe I wanted him to look at me and notice me. I wanted him to realise what he was going to miss.

Yet when I looked in the mirror, I could see my life written into my face. I looked haggard, however much make-up I put on. My nose was too big and my hair looked dull and tired. I've never liked the way I looked, but now I'd give anything for the me I was a couple of years ago.

I'd avoided speaking to him all day, so I didn't know how going out together was going to work. Mind you we'd ignored each other plenty of times in the past and no one had ever noticed. As I walked downstairs, I was practising a nonchalant look that was both

Brown Eyes

normal but gave nothing away. He looked up in surprise.

'Blimey, are we going?' he looked amazed.

'Yes of course we are. We can't let Tania down.'

'I'd better get changed then,' he said.

We got into his car and he drove because he always does. But would he expect me to drive home? I might get incredibly drunk and make him drive.

He was leaning back in his seat and glancing at me, looking rather sheepish. I could tell he was desperate to do the right thing, which made me feel quite powerful. But I couldn't forget what he'd done.

It was strange how you could have a conversation about superficial things in a perfectly polite manner as if you were talking to someone you didn't know very well.

'Have we got a present for Dave?'

'Yes of course. I told you I decided to get him that book on 1970s' sports cars.'

'I remember now. You look nice.'

I wasn't going to answer that. Why do men start complimenting you when they know they're in trouble, and this was worse than trouble? Why didn't he compliment me when things were going OK, if they ever did?

We eased into the road where Tania and Dave lived and although they have lots of

Brown Eyes

space to park around the drive, there were a lot of cars there already.

'Shall I drop you off here and go and park?'

He was being extra gallant. Not the usual Phil.

I got out and stood by the cars waiting for him, not out of any consideration for him. I didn't yet want to bring attention to our separateness. We walked in as if nothing had changed, as if we were the same couple we've always been, but for me we were no longer a couple. We were just two people alongside each other because of circumstance, but we had no reason to be with each other anymore.

I rang the bell and someone I didn't know opened it.

'Come in,' the someone said, and we went in together.

I was relieved that I'd told Tania and Cathy so I had some kind of unspoken support. I saw Dave in the hall as we walked in. I kissed him on the cheek and wandered off into the kitchen to find Tania, leaving Phil chatting to some bloke he seemed to know.

She was looking incredibly voluptuous with a brand-new short haircut and a very low top on, with a huge amount of cleavage showing. It was impossible to not notice, and I found myself staring at her chest, and almost dropped the salad I'd made.

Brown Eyes

Tania put her arms around me, salad and all.

'Merry, so glad you're here. Thanks for the salad. Looks fantastic as ever.'

There was something different about Tania – she just seemed incredibly sexy, and her low plunge top cut across to her arms revealing half of each shoulder. If she wasn't already having a fling with the trainer she soon would be. She oozed sexuality.

'Wow, you look just incredible, Tania.'

'Well, you have to make an effort, don't you darling?'

This was way more than an effort. I could feel someone behind me and it was Dave slipping his arms around me. What was going on with them?

'Where's your other half, Meriel?' Dave asked.

Other half – you'd better ask him who that is, I thought.

'I don't know where he's gone.' I tried to sound nonchalant.

Dave grabbed a bottle of champagne, poured me a glass and turned to Tania and gave her a big kiss.

'It's all due to this wonderful woman. What do you think of her tonight Meriel? I can't keep my hands off her.'

Tania smiled sweetly but deceptively at him,

Brown Eyes

'You've got to entertain your guests, darling.'

Dave wandered off to lech after someone else and I still couldn't be sure what was going on. Then a youngish guy walked into the kitchen. He looked squeaky clean, tall and thin and gorgeous in a boyish sort of way. Tania put her hand on his arm,

'This is Paul, my personal trainer. You know, I told you.'

She was flirting mercilessly and he was looking longingly at her cleavage. He was young enough to be Tania's son – almost.

'I've heard about you, Merry.' He'd even adopted the familiar name that only Tania ever used. I wasn't sure if I liked that.

'When we've been on one of our long runs Tania tells me all about her friends. You're a researcher in TV, aren't you?'

'Yes, I'm afraid I am.'

'Sounds cool.'

He was undoubtedly very charismatic and he seemed incredibly interested in her, but how could you spend time with someone who thinks a job sounds cool? Tania handed him a glass of champagne and gave him that intimate kind of look that speaks volumes.

'I knew Tania had a personal trainer but I didn't know you were coming to the party. Do you know other people here?'

Brown Eyes

'Nope, just Tania. I get to know my clients very well because we spend so much time together working out.'

I almost spat my champagne out and felt like saying, 'I bet you do'.

'What kind of training do you do with people?'

I wanted to laugh, so already this party was doing me good. What with the champagne and this conversation I could have forgotten the awful mess I was in.

'We do a bit of tennis, some running, and some time at the gym doing weights and occasionally we go swimming. It really has to be designed to suit the particular client.'

'Yes, it's certainly working for Tania. She looks really good and much slimmer.'

'Yes,' he says as his eyes run up and down Tania who is standing with her back to us.

I guess it was all down to chemistry. The fact she's a mother of three and is married and must be, what - almost twenty years older than him, maybe none of that mattered. If you'd got that connection with someone, maybe it didn't take any account of age.

Maybe this is what people did these days. Getting divorced seemed to be some badge of honour – one I'd never wanted to have, but it seemed like I'd be joining the club pretty soon myself.

Brown Eyes

Cathy walked in the door with Andy. Cathy had been battling long and hard to fight this bloody disease and she was doing so well. After the operation she'd been told there was no cancer left. I just hoped and prayed that they were right.

'Hi,'

Cathy leant forward and kissed me on both cheeks. Andy looked delighted to see me too. He was such a charming man. I bet he wouldn't cheat on his wife. Especially now he had to think about losing her. Cathy touched my hand lightly.

'Where is he?'

'I don't know, and I don't care. By the way this is Paul, Tania's personal trainer.'

I gave Cathy a knowing look, which she responded to without a flicker on her face to anyone else.

'Hi Paul. I've heard about you,' Cathy said.

'Have you?' He looked chuffed.

Tania turned round and confronted us all with her voluptuous shapeliness. I couldn't blame Paul for looking. I was looking *again*.

Tania flamboyantly kissed Cathy, while glancing sideways at Paul. I'd never ever seen her like this, and I felt jealous. I wanted someone to feel sexy with.

'Wow Tania,' Andy said. 'That husband of yours better keep you on a tight rein.'

Brown Eyes

Tania laughed a bit too enthusiastically and then whisked over to the other side of the room to greet some more guests.

Cathy leant towards me and said in a whisper,

'Is he actually here?'

'Yes, but I'm pretending he's not. How are you? You're looking very well.'

'I am. I can't believe it's a whole year now since I found out, and now I feel much more confident.'

'I'm pleased for you.'

'Thanks. Are you OK?'

'Yes. No. I don't know. I'd like a personal trainer though. That's what I feel at present.'

I heard myself laugh as if it were someone else, and it sounded desperately false. Cathy smiled, nevertheless.

'You never know.'

'Yes, I do. I'm overweight and don't have one ounce of the sexiness that Tania's exuding.'

'I didn't even notice that she had it before, but she certainly has today. Anyway, don't be so down on yourself. I'm sure you could be the same.'

'Chance'd be a fine thing!'

As she laughed, she looked so happy, all the strain of the past few months behind her.

In itself this was something for me to feel joyous about.

5

Benji

I let out a long sigh. I couldn't bear seeing them tearing each other apart like this because I love them. If they carried out their threats, I might not have a home. Supposing they gave me away or forgot all about me and just left me to my own devices.

Meriel is the sweetest person I have ever met but when she was with Phil these days she turned into this nasty vicious woman. They loved each other, I was sure, but they seemed to be destroying it all. I understood that this was getting worse and I was beginning to feel very unhappy and insecure.

They were busy arguing again, and they suddenly stopped and looked at me and laughed.

'Look at Benji – he's gone all miserable because we're rowing.'

Glad to have made them laugh as I hung on to any little ray of hope there might be. I could certainly oblige and look miserable. Perhaps I should look sad or even act ill – would that stop them separating?

Brown Eyes

And had they no thoughts for Ricky and Elly – didn't they have a say in whether their parents decided to go their own separate ways? Surely, they couldn't be so selfish to the ones they loved.

I loved them all deeply and even though Meriel was the one who really cared for me every day I couldn't say either one of them was better than the other. I know more about them than they know about each other because they all talk to me. It was like therapy for them talking to me about their problems, and what's more I see everything.

Just lately I'd been getting worried about Meriel and that guy in the park. Wasn't it too much of a coincidence that every time we went for a walk he was there with that huge boxer of his? I was sure he liked Meriel and because she was in a very vulnerable situation, just one move and she could be his. This was terrifying for me.

Every time I hear my name, I prick up my ears and turn my eyes towards the caller. But I know when my name is being said in a nice way or a horrible way. If it is long and drawn out, a kind of BENNN JEEEE then I'm usually in favour. But on the other hand, if it's too short a quick *Bnji* I might be in trouble.

So, when I heard Meriel shouting loudly,

'What are you doing? You naughty thing.'

Because she hadn't used my name in that cross way, I looked up to see who was in

Brown Eyes

trouble this time and got a shock to find it was me.

'You dirty dog. Look what you've done to my lawn, and I suppose you're looking for a bone or something. Just go inside.'

With my tail firmly between my legs I went inside. This was getting too much now she was shouting at me. I had to see what was under the grass, I didn't know that what I'd done was wrong. I lay down by the French windows and keeping my head down I peeped upwards to see what she was doing.

To my complete dismay Meriel was sitting on a chair weeping – again and it was all my fault this time. I felt so awful that I started to make a slow whining noise because I just couldn't bear to see her like this. Ricky walked in.

'What's the matter with you? Have you lost a bone or something? Do you want to come out and play football?'

I didn't feel at all like going out to play because of what had just happened, but I wanted to try to be nice to all of them. If only he knew how devastating it all was. Ricky walked up to his mum who was just staring in front of her.

'Mum, Mum. You look as if you're miles away – what are you dreaming about? Is it nice?'

Ricky didn't seem to see the worry etched into her face and how pale she looked. I could

Brown Eyes

see it so why couldn't he? He seems very into himself. And he has big spot things on his face, so I think he might be worried that girls are never going to like him. He seems to expect his mum to be there for him all the time as if she didn't have her own feelings and problems.

'I'm going up to the park and I'm taking Benji.'

She looked at me apologetically – at least I thought that's what it was. I moved a bit nearer and she took hold of one of my ears and caressed it. Perhaps she'd forgiven me. I glanced slyly at the mess I had made and wished for one moment that I could put it all back neat and tidy and then she wouldn't have to be upset.

'Look what this naughty dog did.'

She said this in a gentle way and almost smiled.

'Oh, Benji you pain in the butt.'

Ricky wasn't really bothered at all, as long as he didn't have to clear it up.

'I'll get someone to put it back, but I don't know who.'

'Dad, of course.'

'Well, I suppose I could ask him.'

'Whyever not?'

'There's something I ought to tell you.'

'Huh?'

Brown Eyes

Ricky was already disengaged, and he was halfway out of the gate. I ran after him in case he forgot me.

'It will wait,' Meriel mumbled as we disappeared. Once we were on the way, I was relieved to be out away from all the sadness, and it was a great day for smells. I was able to experience being a normal dog for a while with no problems. I ran around sniffing and stopping and then running on again. I bumped into a dog or two and sniffed them the way I like to. It was so relaxing for me to get away for a while.

Ricky was fiddling with his phone as we walked up the path towards the park. I don't mind what he does, but I have noticed that he doesn't talk to me the way he used to. I think he still loves me but he's kind of different. He swears a lot these days too. When he suddenly spoke to me, I was stunned.

'There's something really wrong with my parents Benji. Can't you tell? If they split up, I'm going to live alone without either of them so you can come with me. No rules, plenty of pizza and we can watch TV till we drop.'

6

Benji

After a nice day out, we got back home in time for my tea, and then went to pick up Elly.

'Mum can Kathryn come round for tea, pleeeeease?'

'Yes of course. Get in.'

Ricky didn't speak to Kathryn once, as if she were invisible. I even found it embarrassing but it wasn't helped by Elly saying,

'Ignore my brother. He's at that awkward age.'

Ricky's face was completely blank as if he hadn't even heard what she'd said. We got home and they had tea. He didn't speak all through the meal, and as soon as he'd finished eating, he walked out of the kitchen and ran upstairs. If I had puppies, I wouldn't let them behave so badly.

The music started playing really loudly, and Meriel was tutting and moaning. I wanted to get out of there and I'm sorry to say, away from Meriel. So, I went up to Elly's

Brown Eyes

room and lolled around with the girls, watching them discuss someone who sings and just enjoying their gentle play. I suddenly heard a loud noise in the kitchen and made big strides down the stairs to see what was going on.

There was glass all over the floor.

'Don't come in Benji – no, no!' she called out to me.

Both Phil and Meriel were red in the face and I thought she was going to collapse. How much could one poor person take?

'Sit down or just get out of the kitchen. I'll clear it up. You're in no state to,'

'To what? No state to what Phil?'

'To clear it up – that's all. Stay there Benji.'

Meriel plodded slowly upstairs, and Phil began the task of looking for every tiny bit of glass.

'What can you do with women Benji? You're so much better off. Your relationships are short and sweet, and you can just leave them, and no one calls you a bastard because you find another bitch, do they?'

I was gazing at him to show that I cared and that whatever he had done, even though it was incredibly stupid, I was still here for him. When he'd picked up all the bits he sat down at the table, and I went and lay down on the rug beside him. He picked up that

Brown Eyes

speaking machine and moved his finger over the keypad.

'Hi, do you fancy a drink tonight? Lots going on here and I want to talk to you about it.'

He put the phone down again. I couldn't believe he could be so cruel and disloyal. Perhaps she would be better off without him. I walked out and slumped into my bed and pretended to sleep. He disgusted me.

I was there when Meriel told the children. She called them into the kitchen and made them sit down.

'I've got something to tell you. It's not going to be easy. Dad is moving out.'

Elly screamed,

'What? He's moving out. Why?'

'Don't be stupid Elly,' Ricky retorted. 'Because they don't get on, because they're getting a divorce.'

'How did you know?' Meriel asked.

'What? Is that so? You are getting a divorce?' Elly shrieked.

'No, no, not yet. How did you know Ricky?'

'I could tell. You've been at each other for months now. We never do anything anymore and you're always miserable.'

With that he got up and walked out of the door.

Elly was crying.

Brown Eyes

'I don't want Daddy to go. Why is he going? Doesn't he like us anymore? Does he want a new family?'

'I don't know darling.'

Tania had told Meriel that telling the children would be dreadful. She seemed to be right.

'What do you mean you don't know? Don't you care?'

'Well yes, no, I mean...'

'What do you mean, Mum? Can't you stop him? Won't he listen?'

Meriel said nothing. Was she going to tell her daughter that he wanted to stay, but it was her that wouldn't let him?

'Won't he listen?'

'It's too complicated. It's all very grown up and I don't know if you can understand.'

'Has he got someone else? Have you?'

'I just don't know.'

She might not have known, but I heard the phone call. I let out a squeal and they looked at me, but obviously they didn't know why. I went to lie down in the corner so these involuntary noises would stop. I'd be better if I was asleep, but Elly had other ideas.

'Come on Benji,' she said in a high-pitched voice. 'Come with me.'

She took me into her room and let me get on the bed, a real treat, and something her mother normally forbade.

Brown Eyes

And then she sort of lay across me as if I were a giant pillow.

'I don't understand Benji. My dad wants to go away, and my mum doesn't seem to care. I'm sick of adults and their stupid behaviour. Why can't they get their lives together instead of trying to ruin ours? You're staying with me because I love you more than them anyway.'

The music from Ricky's room was louder than ever but Meriel obviously didn't dare go in and say anything. He was so quiet and grunty these days, but now he had something to be quiet about.

Phil moved out into a small place, which wasn't very suitable for me so I didn't go with him, nor did I even visit.

He took two suitcases and went, and every Saturday he came back to see the children and I'd like to think he came for me too, but he didn't really. Elly was quite friendly towards him but Ricky seemed to make up excuses every time he came.

'Can't come, I'm playing football. Got too much homework. Not feeling well.'

All excuses and not very good ones at that. If he'd wanted to see his dad he could have done so.

Meriel seemed to be trying to put a brave face on it and she kept walking me when she knew that man with the retriever would be around. I was almost getting to be offhand with the dog because I was so bothered about

Brown Eyes

them getting too friendly. I mean if they started a relationship, there'd be no going back at all.

They sat on the bench together with the backdrop of the palm trees. Kids were playing on the skateboard park, while he told her about his wife leaving him two years earlier. She sounded all silly and sympathetic. Then she told him about Phil and how he'd been off with this girl at work. This made him touch her arm. I growled and watched. She turned to me and laughed, not sounding like herself at all.

When he brushed her hand, I moved nearer to her. They laughed again, which rather annoyed me.

'Do you think he's jealous?' the man called Jack said.

She smiled as if she liked him. He put his hand over hers and said,

'I'd like to take you out to dinner one evening if that's OK.'

I couldn't take that and I barked. I couldn't help it, it just came out. They both laughed again. And he said,

'If your dog allows you to, of course.'

'I'm sure he will.'

I whined but I wanted to stamp my paws and howl. They obviously didn't understand how I felt because they giggled again as if they were children, and he patted my head. I

Brown Eyes

quickly moved, but nothing I did was any good because they arranged the dinner, when the kids would be with Phil. This was the end.

7

Benji

It was quite amazing how human lives could completely change and everyone suddenly thought they were normal – well the adults did. I don't for one minute believe that Elly and Ricky were totally happy with the situation. Their mother was seeing this man every few weeks for dinner and they didn't like that for starters, and whatever their father did they didn't know.

I wasn't happy with any of it. I knew that Phil and Meriel loved each other, so what was the point in her starting to see this other man? It wasn't right and I didn't want to let her think I was happy about it. Every time she got dressed up and looked beautiful, I made a big fuss whining and creating so that she wouldn't go out, but it didn't work at all.

Ricky was old enough to babysit now so she just went and left the three of us together. One night when she was out Ricky came out of his room and joined Elly in the lounge.

'Do you think Mum's seeing a man?' Elly asked her brother.

Brown Eyes

'Huh, she doesn't get all dolled up to go to yoga, does she?'

'So, she is?'

'Pretty much,' Ricky sneered.

'Don't you like it?'

'Course I fucking don't. Do you?'

'No but there's no need to swear is there?'

'Shut up, don't be so prudish. I'm sick of them both, mucking up our lives, changing everything and ruining it. Everything was fine before they went and screwed it up.'

'I know. What can we do? I mean is there a way of making them get back together?'

'They're f—ing grown-ups and they do what they like. We don't get a say do we?'

'Now you're swearing again. But you're right, whoever asked us what we wanted? It makes me sick. They are so selfish. Did I ask to have my parents going out with other people and screwing up our lives? Did I?'

'Well maybe they just don't know what they're doing.'

'But they're supposed to be the ones who do know what they're doing. How come they keep telling us what we should do if they're so dumb? Do you think Dad was seeing someone else?'

'What screwing someone?'

'Well, yes. Do you have to put it like that?'

'Course. That's what blokes do don't they?'

Brown Eyes

'I'm never getting married if that's what they do. I want my husband to just love me and never look at anyone else.'

'That doesn't happen anymore. That's back with your fairy tales. Now they all get divorced. You know at school – half the class has divorced parents. Perhaps it's cool, the thing to do so that's why they do it. I don't care.'

'But you just said you did.'

'I don't anymore. I just don't want her bringing some tosser back here.'

'He might be all right.'

'He won't be and anyway it's too soon.'

The phone rang and it was their dad.

'Hi Dad. No, she's out. Where? I think some man's taken her out to dinner. Sorry, perhaps I shouldn't have said that. Ricky's here.

'He hung up. I don't think he liked my saying that.'

'Course he didn't – what did he say?'

'She's what? Really crossly.'

'As if it's any of his business, the bastard.'

'Look Daddy still loves you, and me for that matter.'

'How do you know?'

'Cos he told me. And I believe him. Why shouldn't he? We're his kids.'

'He should have thought of that before, shouldn't he?'

Brown Eyes

Later on, when Elly was asleep and Ricky was watching people kicking a ball around on the box in his room, Meriel came in with that man. They were laughing and giggling, and I was getting very uneasy when he took hold of her and started kissing her. This time I kept quiet because I thought they'd think I was a stupid dog if I reacted.

'I've been wanting to do that for some time,' he told Meriel, and she turned back to him and kissed him again.

Before they'd even made coffee, they were on the sofa with each other, and you couldn't tell them apart. I felt as if I shouldn't be there, so I closed my eyes, but I kept opening one to see what they were up to next. I was worried that this was getting serious.

'No Jack. Not now. It's too soon.'

Good. She'd given him his marching orders.

'I'll make some coffee.'

What a relief – they stopped behaving like a pair of animals and started talking to each other. She put on some slow music and went to make the coffee. When she came back, she sat opposite him which was much better, and he politely stood up and said,

'I must go.'

Then he started kissing her again and I got very uneasy so this time I stood up and walked over slowly and quietly. Jack looked

Brown Eyes

up and I was peering into his face. He
jumped.

'Someone's jealous again,' Jack mumbled
and as he lunged at her again, I just stood
right by them.

'I'll let him in the garden. Thanks so much
for tonight. It's meant a lot to me,' Meriel told
him. This I didn't want to hear.

8

Meriel

'Deep down I feel that you love each other, and I find it really hard to see you throwing away the life you have together with love, that is so rare to find for anyone.'

Why was it that Tania always got right to the heart of the matter and knew exactly what to say? She was completely right, of course we loved each other. I knew that deep inside, but what could I do?

I have this block, this inability to say to him, 'I was wrong. Let's give it another go. I forgive you. Forget the past. Let's start anew.'

I just couldn't do that.

'Never forget the love there is within your family. Whatever happens it's still there. Couldn't you just swallow your pride and try and get him back before it's too late?'

'No.'

'Why?'

'I don't know. It's so hard. My pride seems to get in the way, it seems like a block. I just can't get past it.'

Brown Eyes

'You are throwing away a wonderful life and a wonderful man because of pride. Isn't it time you let go of it? Surely that's not so valuable to you, is it?'

She sounded so irritated I wondered if I was pissing her off.

'I can't trust a man who was unfaithful to me. It will never be the same.'

'And how was it?'

'Not very good.'

'So do you want it to be the same?'

'No.'

'Did you trust him before?'

'No, yes, well no. I suppose not.'

'So why not try to get the trust now?'

'How?'

'You need to go and talk to someone, the two of you.'

'What about Laura? Aren't you forgetting about her?'

'She's a diversion, Meriel. Men like to comfort themselves with sex, don't they? She's simply a diversion. It's you he loves. You can see it in his eyes. I've always seen it – he's the one who adores you, and it's you who maybe doesn't feel so strongly.'

'Mmm. You may be right.'

I was blushing, but I didn't know why.

'It's none of my business of course, but I want to see you happy.'

Brown Eyes

'I know. I know. I'll think about it. But how do you get rid of the habits of a lifetime? How do I let go of these awful burdens like pride and fear and mistrust?'

'You take steps to do so. You have to work it out. You have to go and talk to someone.'

'Not counselling, that's not for me Tania.'

'Why not?'

'Because I'm too cynical. It's just not for me.'

'Meriel you can stay cynical and proud for the rest of your life, but you might have to accept that you are going to be miserable too. On that happy note I am going to leave you but don't forget, I love you and I wouldn't bother saying all this if I didn't.'

She enveloped me in her arms, which made me feel safe and nurtured.

9

Meriel

I couldn't see Benji anywhere.

'Elly, Elly have you seen Benji?

'Nope.'

I ran to the stairs and called up,

'Ricky is Benji with you?'

'Naaa.'

'Benji, Benji come here.'

Normally he bounded out of the bushes and came over tail wagging, looking so happy and welcoming, but today there was no black beast to be seen. Confident that he'd be lurking at the back of the garden shed seeking out a fox or chasing the neighbour's cat, I put my boots on and went out.

'Come on Benji, stop mucking about.' Why was I talking to him as if he were a person?

'Look I'm in a hurry. Benji.'

An unpleasant feeling came into the pit of my stomach. Life was so bloody difficult at present. I just didn't have time to run around looking for a naughty dog. And, what if he was gone? Of course, he wasn't.

Brown Eyes

At the end of the lawn, I stood by the bushes and went back to where the trees provided cover for a dog as dark as Benji. He could be sniffing around in here oblivious to my calls. He wasn't though.

I stood still by the back fence peering over to the estuary beyond. Not a soul of human or canine kind. Then I saw it – the hole in the fence, the one that Phil had never really fixed in four years. He'd gone through it and who knew where he was now? My stomach turned over and I felt rigid with fear.

I made myself run back to the house, grabbed my coat and called,

'I've gone to look for Benji.'

No one offered to help me, so I ran up the garden path and through the old gate which had been jammed closed for so long that it took a heavy push for me to open it.

In the distance I could hear a football match in progress – Benji had spent years on the touch line so perhaps he'd decided to go and chase the ball. He would be there, I was sure.

As I drew nearer to the football, I could hear all this cursing. 'F—g bollocks, f— off,' and so it went on. What was the matter with young men that they couldn't move an inch without letting out a filthy stream of language? Everyone swore these days, and I am not averse to the odd four-letter word, but what if you had an old maiden aunt or a

Brown Eyes

three-year-old with you? Do they want to hear this kind of thing?

For a moment my mind was on the foul-mouthed footballers, so I momentarily forgot the purpose of the whole escapade and it was with a sickening thud that I remembered that I was after our beautiful family dog whom everybody loved so much. What would the kids do if he was gone? They'd already lost Phil and now Benji.

I saw a tail wagging in the distance. Oh, please be Benji, but it wasn't. It was a sheepdog, not a dog who was going to smile at me when he saw me. I ran around past the football onlookers asking manically,

'Has anyone seen a black Labrador?'

Most people ignored me as if I were just a neurotic middle-aged woman, but one or two people asked a few questions. They were just being nice. Was he black all over? Was he young?

'You want to watch them dogs,' an old chap helpfully told me. 'They sell 'em you know, those bloody gypsies.'

I knew, I'd heard about it, but this was the last thing I wanted to be reminded of. My friend Jane had told me about a red setter who disappeared. Apparently, they set up dog fights in the park or took out lots of dogs so that yours got lost in the melée. Then they whipped it away while you were confused or trying to prevent yourself from being bitten.

Brown Eyes

This poor woman's setter disappeared, and she made all these investigations to find it.

Eventually she found out who had it and when she got there it was dead. They killed it rather than let her have it back.

How could my family take that, after all the heartache? I just couldn't cope. I was going into panic mode and my stomach felt like it wanted to burst. I started to cry.

'Benji. Please don't go,' I called out, but started running home. I ran back, the tears coursing down my face, consumed with fear. Nothing else mattered in that moment, I just wanted Benji back. What would I tell the children? When I got back in the house Elly was looking out of the window and Ricky was putting his trainers on to come outside.

Elly wailed, 'Haven't you got him, Mum? No, where is Benji?'

I couldn't deal with my daughter's grief and panic. I was feeling so pathetic these days that I just didn't have the reserves I used to be able to muster up.

'Mum.'

Ricky looked kindly at me, a look I see so rarely these days among the grunting and ignoring that has become the norm of my adolescent boy. He normally just complained and moaned if something wasn't to his liking or he didn't speak at all.

Brown Eyes

It was too much seeing him be so nice. My eyes filled with tears but I didn't want him to see.

'I just don't know Ricky – what to do...'

My sentence tailed off and I felt deflated, defeated and depressed all at one.

I shouldn't crumple because I am Mum and I'm here to fix everything but Ricky took charge.

'You go in and have a cup of tea,' my son told me. 'I'm going out to look. Don't worry.'

Underneath it all he was a lovely boy. Why did it always have to be drastic circumstances that brought it on?

'I'll find him. Don't worry.'

It was as if he had grown into a man all in the last five minutes. He was taking care of me and I needed that.

'Can I ring Dad?' Elly asked as I walked into the house. She looked like a frightened little girl. I slumped on the bed defeated. I didn't want him involved in anything. He'd broken up our family. But I didn't have the strength to say 'no' to Elly. Even in my panic I could see that Phil was Elly's dad and she wanted him to know about the crisis, and besides he loved Benji almost more than anyone else, except.... Don't even go there.

I heard Elly in the other room.

Brown Eyes

'Dad, Benji's gone missing. It's pretty awful. Mum's been up through the park and Ricky's out now. Have you seen him?'

Why Phil should have seen him five miles away I couldn't imagine.

'I'll get her now.'

She walked in with the phone and said,

'He wants to speak to you.'

After three months of avoiding him every time he rang, by not answering the phone or leaving it on voicemail, I was caught on the hop and couldn't think of an excuse. Deep down I needed to speak to him, to have him reassure me.

His voice was soothing, and I had a recollection of how tender he could be.

'Are you OK, Meriel?'

This was the last straw. First my son and now my estranged husband being nice to me, and for a moment I forgot how much I despised him for going off with Laura and ruining my life.

My voice was little and stupid, and I just mustered,

'I suppose so.'

'You don't sound it.'

Why was he being so nice? I could feel it all welling up inside, my childhood when my dogs and cats were lost and died and how I just had to shrug off my grandfather's death although I adored him. The sorrow of losing

Brown Eyes

my father, the devastation of losing Phil, and now Benji.

'I just can't....'

I was fighting back the tears so much that it was hurting my throat and I couldn't speak. Elly was standing watching me, so I turned my head the other way and put my hand on my brow cradling the phone in my neck.

'I'll be over.'

Ricky walked into the lounge with his trainers all dirty, dropping bits of mud on the carpet. Normally I'd scream at him but I just looked on helplessly. What did it really matter anyway? The carpet could be cleaned, but our shattered life couldn't.

'I've been everywhere,' he sounded really cross.

Cross with Benji, cross with whom?

'I've been to the neighbour's and up to the shops, up and down the roads and he's nowhere. He's just vanished. I went round to that couple's who've got the two dogs he loves, and they haven't seen him.'

The three of us stood there and I felt powerless – gone was the mother who mopped up after everyone. I felt like a quivering jelly and had no ability to mop up for anyone else, but this was life and they had to face it too. I couldn't make everything right.

The doorbell went and Elly's face lit up,

Brown Eyes

'Daddy.'

The thought crossed my mind that maybe Elly would rather be with Phil than me because she loved him so much. Ricky had been totally off Phil since it happened, but he even looked pleased to see him. No wonder - when their mother was falling apart, they needed someone to be a rock.

He looked really nice but... Like electricity the thought that he'd been in bed with that woman again stabbed my heart and made me feel like I was subsiding completely.

'I'll make a cup of coffee,' I said and stumbled into the kitchen. I breathed deeply in an attempt to get myself back together again.

I could hear him talking in the other room.

'Has Mum rung the police?'

As if the police had time to look for lost dogs these days. He came into the kitchen.

'When did you last see him?'

'Well, I suppose it was this morning. He had his breakfast, but he's been a bit miserable lately.'

Just like me, I was thinking, so I didn't want to continue along these lines.

'I'll ring Pet Rescue and the police, OK?'

He smiled sweetly but I couldn't meet his eyes. I felt so pathetic. I wanted Phil to think that I was over him now, that I was having a

Brown Eyes

great life, that I had a new man, and I did, almost.

He spent the next hour with the children and I pottered around in the kitchen, keeping out of his way. I turned round from putting something in the cupboard and he was just there moving in to put his arms around me. That was too much to cope with and I couldn't stop the tears from coming, and he held me tightly while I wept. I just hoped that he was thinking that the tears were all for Benji.

The way he held me reminded me of how he used to be gentle, and we used to be close, before everything went wrong, and we became more and more distant. I had forgotten how gentle he could be.

He was stroking my hair, holding me as if he had everything under control.

'We're all hurting Meriel.'

'I can't take any more. It's too much.'

All that strength I'd gathered together in the last few months had evaporated and now I was in his arms like a weakling unable to resist or to stand firm.

Ricky walked in, looked horrified, and went straight out again. How confusing for a kid to see his estranged parents locked in embrace. How was he to understand what it meant? But nor did I.

10

Benji

I considered staying away forever but in reality, it wasn't that easy. Often when Meriel walked me over the fields I played with some of the dogs at the farm. I knew the way very well, but I was trying to make a statement. It was like I had got to the point where I didn't know what I was going to do to change the situation, so I decided to disappear. Somehow the house just wasn't the same and I wanted to get away. In the back of my mind was the faint hope that this would make a difference.

I found the boxer dog, Rosie, the bitch I really liked and I knew she liked me too. During the day it was no problem at all. I played with the dogs and the tall greyhound with fluffy, furry type hair chased me up and down for fun and Rosie and I licked and kissed each other. No one batted an eyelid all day but at night the other dogs were called in and they told me to go. I'd scratched off my collar because I didn't want to be found, and now I regretted it. I wondered if I could find it and drop it in front of them.

Brown Eyes

One of the farm girls came over to talk to me.

'You're a lovely dog but you must go home now.'

She bent down to look for my name.

'No collar. That's a problem. I wonder if you're microchipped.'

She walked me to the gate and pointed down the lane.

'Go home now.'

I didn't know what to do, so I pretended to walk off and then when they turned round, I ran back in through the gate and up to the hay barn. I could sleep in there and be quite warm and no one would even notice.

Hugo was watching me, and I was terrified he would bark and give the game away, but he kept quiet and just looked. I nodded at him to show appreciation and went into the hay barn. It was cosy and smelt of mice which I liked.

During the night I kept waking up. In fact, I hardly slept at all. I had never spent a night outside and I was all alone and wishing I was in my bed at home with my family. I started wondering if they'd miss me and was I being unkind doing this to them? All I really wanted now was to be found, but I felt rather stupid and didn't know whether to trot home nonchalantly as if nothing had happened.

Brown Eyes

In the morning the dogs came and found me again and I had a whole morning of running around and kissing and licking Rosie. I forgot about my circumstances and my regrets when I was with her. I heard someone say that they ought to call the dog police because my owners might be worried about me. It was strange but I tried not to care about them, because I felt they'd disrupted my life and I was running away from it.

I kept hiding every time I thought a car turned up because I didn't really want to leave. I decided that this was the life for me. Provided I could eat the other dogs' food I would be quite happy here.

Later that day I heard my name being called which was odd as no one knew it. I went and hid round the corner and then I heard my family talking. Meriel kept saying,

'I so hope it's him. We miss him so much.'

And then I heard Phil's voice. 'How long has he been there?'

'Dad please let it be Benji,' Elly said.

Perhaps Phil was back home and everything would be all right again.

I couldn't resist peering round the corner and immediately I saw them. Meriel looking terribly worried, Ricky and Elly running around looking for me, and Phil just as he used to be. I forgot all about my reasons for running away, about the unhappiness, the awful atmosphere and Meriel's dull moods,

Brown Eyes

and the builder she was seeing, and I just ran hell for leather across the farmyard.

'Benji,' Rick yelled out. 'Look it's him.'

I was so excited my tail kept wagging and they almost let me jump up they were so pleased to see me. Meriel burst into tears, quite why I couldn't work out as she had found me now. Phil put his arm round her, and I stood there for a moment with my tongue hanging out, not believing what I was seeing.

They all fussed over me so much I thought it was well worth running away. I hadn't been having a lot of attention since the separation and this reminded me what it was like when I was a little puppy and the centre of their world. They were stroking and kissing me and bending down to hug me. I loved them so much, what had I been thinking of?

'I guess he's your dog then?' Mr. Blatch, the farmer said, and they all laughed as if he had made a really funny joke.

'He came and found us again,' Elly said. 'Do you remember, Rick, that's how we got him because he raced up to us and chose us when he was just an eight-week-old puppy?'

I ran up to Phil's car and jumped into the boot and we set off home. I hoped against hope that he had moved back in, and everything was going to be completely normal from then on. I felt a warm glow and a sense

Brown Eyes

of happiness. I suppose you didn't appreciate anything until you had nearly lost it.

I thought of Rosie and gave a big sigh, because she was a beautiful bitch, but nothing can beat being at the heart of your own family.

At home I was given an excellent meal of chicken and biscuits and then I curled up in my own basket and went to sleep. Phil was still there, and I was sure that everything was going to be OK for good now.

When I woke up, I kept my eyes half-closed so I could assess the situation.

'I know it's silly,' Meriel was saying. 'But when something like this happens you forget your differences and you just want to be together.'

I looked up and, as I suspected, she was on the red liquid again.

'It made me think,' she carried on, 'What would I do if something happened to you? Or supposing something happened to me?'

'I would never forgive myself Meriel. I still want us to be together you know. We are a family. Benji going makes me realise that. I just wish we could try again.'

I felt almost puffed up, that I could have had such a result. Perhaps it had all been worthwhile.

Brown Eyes

Meriel was smiling and said really softly. 'I'd like that, but how do we do it? You're seeing Laura and I'm...'

'You are what?' he said, not harshly.

'Um, um, I've started rebuilding my life. I've got someone I see occasionally too.'

Why did she have to say that? He looked crestfallen.

'Hmm, I didn't know. Is it serious?'

I could just imagine how he felt inside, just how I felt when Hugo went and tried to get on to Rosie.

'Not yet. He's good to me Phil.'

'Well, the situation has reversed.'

'What do you mean?'

'I'm not seeing Laura anymore.'

'Really?' She sounded delighted. 'Why not?'

'It didn't work out and because I couldn't really give her anything when all I wanted was to be with you. Once I was away from home, I realised what I wanted more than anything. And I know it sounds ridiculous but being with someone who wants to listen to Radio 1 when I'd rather have Radio 4 on was beginning to irritate me. I guess the age difference was showing.'

He moved nearer to her on the sofa and I was so pleased it wasn't that builder bloke she was seeing. I had to shift my head slightly to watch what was going on because they'd gone

Brown Eyes

quiet. I could hear this sound and saw their mouths were together. I had to hold all my strange noises inside, because I was so excited. All I wanted to do was leap up and bark but that would interrupt them.

'Who is this man?' he asked her, and she looked like she was enjoying this bit of jealousy.

'You don't know him. He's a builder who lives in East Carstead
. He's just a friend really.'

I nearly snorted. He didn't look like a friend the other night, that dreadful night when he was pawing her, and she only just turned him away before bedtime.

'Perhaps we should talk about it,' Meriel said. There's been a lot wrong with our relationship I know. I blamed you completely for going off with Laura, but we had become very distanced, and I wasn't really giving you what you wanted. And people don't run off with someone else unless something is wrong.'

It was obvious this was the drink talking because Meriel would never be so humble normally.

'The way I feel now, since I've lost you all, the kids and even that silly old dog.'

Thanks a lot.

'I don't want to be a divorce statistic and I'll do anything to get back with you, for us all to be together. I have to say this Meriel, I'm

Brown Eyes

sorry but I now see that I went off with Laura because you weren't very interested in me, I felt. She showed an interest and I was weak, and I wish I hadn't, but I did.

'And there's this kind of illicit excitement when you're married. I shouldn't say this to you, but I'm trying to be honest.

'And when I was with her and available there was no excitement. In fact, there was nothing. When it's for real it's a completely different deal.

'She is a nice girl, but she kept asking me if I'd seen you and the kids, and I felt hemmed in by her. I didn't need that. I just want us to be together right now.'

'Hang on,' obviously Meriel hadn't had too much drink. 'You can't just move in Phil, and we start again. It doesn't work like that. It will all go wrong again. We need to do some work.'

'Yep. I'll do some work, anything.' He stroked her hair again, but she wasn't thrown off course.

'We need to go to see someone.'

'Who?'

'I won't go back unless we sort it out because it could happen again. I've got to find some trust again. We need to find a way forward.'

'If that's what you feel.'

'I do.'

Brown Eyes

'I'll do it. You're probably right, you usually are.'

'What shall we tell the kids?'

'The truth? That we're meeting each other and trying to resolve things.'

'And that they might not work out.'

'Be positive Meriel, for Christ's sake.'

'Ricky misses you so much and I think he blames me because it was me who wanted you to go. And he's a man.'

'Hardly fair.'

'He's fourteen and he identifies more with his dad than me, and males rule in his world.'

'He adores you.'

'That's not too obvious at present. And Elly – well I sometimes wonder if she'd rather be with you than me.'

'Don't be silly, a twelve year old girl needs her mother.'

'Yes. The plain truth is that they would both prefer to be with both of us. That's how kids are isn't it?'

'Have they said anything about it at all?'

'No not much but I'm concerned about Elly. The reports from school are that she's not trying as hard.'

'And Ricky?'

'Same as usual. He isn't mad about working but I guess he's doing OK. Who knows what goes on in a teenage mind? They're more concerned about their spots,

Brown Eyes

their friends, which girls or boys they like. It's just an added complication, an embarrassment I expect.'

'We should do it for their sake, and ours then.'

'Yes Phil.'

'Can I stay tonight?'

'No, we can't start off like that. We need more time to recapture our relationship. I can't just do that.'

'I could right now.'

She smiled.

'I get the impression you're turning me out in the cold.'

'Fraid so. We have to do this properly.'

'Yes. I do want you back Meriel, not just for the sake of the children, or the dog.'

'I don't know,' she said. 'Maybe it's too late and we've moved on and I'm seeing someone else now. Perhaps this is how it's meant to be.'

My head dropped on to my paws. I couldn't believe this woman. What made her say that? She so obviously loves him and what was she doing but putting him off and all for that stupid other man? Why, oh why? Didn't she want to be happy?

Phil put on his coat and, 'Suit yourself,' and left. What a stupid woman. I decided I wasn't going to have anything to do

Brown Eyes

with her any more, so that she came to her senses.

As soon as he closed the door, she sat down next to me and it was just too difficult to ignore her when she took my head between her hands. She looked directly into my eyes and started talking to me.

'Life's so complicated Benji. Why did it all have to turn out like this? But he went off with someone else and it's too late now.'

Never have I wished I could communicate as much as at that moment. Why didn't she patch it up with Phil so we could be a happy family all over again? What was it with humans that they hurt each other so much instead of having a good fight and biting each other's legs and then getting on again? With dogs you knew where you were.

I could see deep into her eyes as if I were looking into her soul. I didn't want her to think this was sympathy, but I hoped she understood what I wanted to convey – that they loved each other, and she was throwing away a chance of happiness, not just for herself but for everyone, and me too.

'You are lovely,' she said to me. 'You're the one who understands me.'

Unfortunately, I didn't – my life could never be as complicated as hers.

There used to be so much love in this family. When I heard about other families that dogs live with, there's so much hurt

Brown Eyes

people inflict on each other. I always felt so smug and satisfied that I had the good fortune to be with people who never behaved like that.

I could never have known how wrong everything was going, and how the relationship between Meriel and Phil almost destroyed us all.

Maybe it was that hate was so close to love that when love went sour, people were much more cruel to each other than they would ever be to another human being. But who were they trying to hurt? Life was so much simpler with us dumb animals.

The Stevensons weren't very rich but they had cars and holidays and nice clothes. And then there's me. I'm not a mongrel so people knew that they were able to afford a dog with a substantial pedigree.

I heard Meriel telling someone about my name one day, 'Anyway it's better than Billy Buster, which is what he was called when he chose us.'

The other woman started laughing like mad and I didn't know whether to be offended or not.

But I was chuffed that Meriel should say 'chose us' because I did. Several people had been to look at me, but the Stevensons were just right for me. I ran out and played with Ricky as soon as I saw him, whereas my sister

Brown Eyes

hid under the chair which is great because they might have taken her if she hadn't.

This family knew how to treat a dog, I could tell, and they were much better than all the other ones I'd met. They went away to make a decision and I thought they'd forget all about me, but they didn't. They came back for me.

I don't want to give the impression that I wanted to leave my mummy and my sister because I didn't. I loved them a lot, but this is what puppies do and I had to go, so why not choose a great family?

I cried for a couple of days, and they were all so lovely to me that I knew I'd made the right decision and then sadly I forgot my mummy and sister and got on with my new life with the Stevensons. Now I wonder if it was so good after all.

11

Benji

Grandma Ethel was lovely to the children and the rest of the world and people thought that she was a delightful old lady. She wasn't like that with Meriel though. She was so critical of her it almost amounted to cruelty.

Meriel had asked her over for a 'spot of lunch' and I was lying nearby feeling protective towards her from the onslaught of her mother's vicious tongue.

As they started eating their goat's cheese salad and washing it down with a glass of red liquid, Meriel started nervously.

'Mum, I've got something to tell you…'

She cut her off before she'd started.

'You're giving up work. About time too I say. Those poor children – latchkey kids – having to put up with a mother who's working all the time.'

She was so fast with her tongue that it was hard for my Meriel to get a word in. In fact, she was going all red in the face as if she was terrified.

Brown Eyes

'Mum, please listen. It's more serious than that.'

'I hope it's not about you and Phil.'

'It is.'

'What's happened? You haven't upset him, have you?'

'He's moved out.'

Grandma almost forgot how old she was and leapt out of her seat.

'He's what? Why? What have you done?'

'Why should it be me who's done something? What the bloody hell do you think, he's some kind of saint or something?'

'No need to swear dear. I like Phil.'

'Well, your precious Phil has been unfaithful.'

'Oh, is that all?'

'Is that all?' I thought Meriel would explode. She blurted the words out so loudly that I almost jumped and decided to move out of the firing line and observe from a distance. I sat up and looked at her so she knew that I was there for her, watching over her.

'What do you mean is that all? Unfaithful – do you even know what it means?'

The gloves were off now.

'Of course I do. Don't forget who your father was dear. Has he gone off with this woman?'

'No.'

'So why has he gone?'

Brown Eyes

'Because I cannot live with him. He's an adulterer.'

'Forgive me saying dear,' she was sounding nice and that was even more worrying. 'But that's a bit of an old-fashioned term, and attitude actually. You need a man to look after you.'

'I don't. I don't need a man, particularly one who can't keep himself to himself.'

'But were you giving him what he wanted?'

'That's none of your business.'

'But it might be relevant, dear. You know men have their needs.'

Meriel looked at the ceiling. Why was it her mother seemed to think she had no experience of life at all?

'With respect, Mum,' she said sarcastically. 'I've been around a lot of men you know.'

'I'm not sure I want to know that. Have you got someone else?'

'I've got an interest.'

'Who in, may I ask?'

'Um, his name is Jack, and he's a builder.'

'No, no, no, no, no, no.' That is a word I understand very well. Why did her mother have to say so many no's'? She always did and it made her seem more and more like a schoolteacher telling Meriel what to do.

'A builder. For goodness' sake Meriel.'

Brown Eyes

'What do you mean, for goodness' sake? He's a very nice man, a kind man. Don't be such a snob.'

'I'm not, but can a builder really look after you?'

'Yes, if you hadn't noticed. They earn heaps of money and quite frankly mother it's the latest thing. Women are sick and tired of having husbands who can't fix anything, so they are all running off with builders. Barb at work did and you remember Yvonne, she has. It's a very practical idea.'

I couldn't agree with this at all. Meriel was going a bit too far and this seemed like a very strange defence in the face of the enemy.

'Well, it may be, but just because I want a pint of milk every day doesn't mean I have to live with the milkman.'

'Look mother. He's just a friend. I'm not at that stage yet. One relationship is barely over.'

'I can't help thinking that one infidelity is nothing. Women have to put up with that sort of thing. It's much better than being alone, isn't it?'

'No. This is the 21st century, not the Dark Ages. Women have careers and they are independent, not like when you were young. We don't put up with men mucking you around I'm afraid. We've been liberated. Have you not seen the news? Women run the world now.'

Brown Eyes

Her voice was rising and her face was getting even more red.

Grandma Ethel threw back her head and scoffed.

'You give me liberation. No woman is liberated where men are concerned. That's our lot in life and it's time you realised it.'

Very calmly Meriel turned to her and said,

'Thank you so much for your support. I know I can always count on it and that's all I ever want.'

Her mother smiled ever so sweetly,

'Of course, darling. You are my daughter after all.'

12

Meriel

Things went from bad to worse. Whenever Phil appeared we didn't really speak. One day he drove up in his car and Benji, who was in the garden, bounded up to the gate. Phil came to the door with Elly's sunglasses but the kids were out and he didn't seem keen to come in, hung around outside and then said goodbye. He seemed in a hurry to get away, but as he was walking back down the path, I remembered I needed to ask for him some money for Ricky's rugby trip.

I got to the gate and looked up at the car and froze. There was a young woman sitting in the front seat and I knew immediately it was her. My mouth was open as if I was about to form a word when Phil, who was climbing into the car, turned and saw me. He blushed and had that really sheepish look he gets when he feels guilty and embarrassed. He got out again to move towards me, but I dashed inside. I couldn't bear the humiliation.

I ran into the house and slammed the door and Phil just left. Was he a liar then or did he

Brown Eyes

go back to this Laura because I had rejected him?

I could feel the raw emotion in my stomach. It felt as if he just existed to hurt me. Did I still love him? That's what Tania thinks and sometimes I wondered if it was true.

It's like I didn't want him, but I didn't want anyone else to have him. Maybe I just wanted him to be on his own pining for me, not making up for losing this family with someone else. It hurt all the more, particularly because he'd told me that he wasn't seeing Laura anymore. If it were Laura – how am I to know? There could be a whole string of women.

I still had Jack, but I had been holding off because I suppose I still wanted the chance of Phil coming back if he wasn't seeing Laura.

I've been having so much trouble with the kids. Being a single mother seemed like such an impossible job because everything you did was wrong. They expected the house to run like clockwork while they put all manner of obstacles in the way. It was as if they wanted to trick me out and then show me that everything I did was imperfect. It wasn't a hotel – why should it be perfect?

I would spend two hours tidying and cleaning and after ten minutes of Ricky and Elly being home there were three pairs of shoes thrown around the lounge, a pair of dirty football boots at the bottom of the stairs

Brown Eyes

surrounded by large chunks of mud, a pile of school bags in the middle of the floor in the kitchen and crumbs and dirty glasses in the kitchen.

What was the point in bothering? All I did was nag them because I was trying desperately to keep some level of orderliness, but they didn't want that. It's me that wanted it, so was I neurotic or is that I just needed the order in my life to make me feel in control?

They didn't appreciate me at all. They looked in the fridge and moaned if there wasn't something to their liking.

It's a perennial problem and both Cathy and Tania say it happened to them. In fact, all the women I know seemed to have a complicit understanding of what it's like having teenagers. How not to be a nag, but keep on top of things? Was I to be a doormat and run round after everyone or a harridan and keep following them around asking them to pick up, clean up, tidy up?

Phil never had to worry about any of this. He just picked them up, took them out for a few hours, had a lovely time and dropped them back. He never had worried about it, because he left it all to me to cope with the mess and he used to always ask me what all the fuss was about.

I read a book about a man who looked after his kids when his wife died. Halfway

Brown Eyes

through he said he'd turned into a woman. He no longer wanted the mess, the chaos, the take-away pizzas, because he'd become civilised and now he was in charge, he just nagged the whole time.

Today's woman was said to have it all, and it was right. I'd got it all – the hassle of keeping down a job and earning money and the hassle of running a home, but with far less time than my mother ever had. And given the choice about which I preferred, the work won every time.

Not that I haven't wanted to spend time with Elly and Ricky, but how much better to have someone clear it all up – a permanent maid, or even better a wife? How many successful women could do with a wife who sorted everything out for them while they worked?

When Jack touched me such strong feelings of sadness came over me that I thought I would cry. It made me realise how lonely I was, how much I missed the intimacy of a relationship, that I felt I hadn't had for so long, well before the crisis with Phil. I didn't want Jack to know I was crying but it was strange because my whole body felt love towards him for just being there for me, and the sadness welled up from the memories of a lost past.

The last time I felt this close to someone was back in the dim and distant past, before

Brown Eyes

we had children, when we weren't even married.

And before that with the other one I'd loved and lost as well. Why was I so hopeless at this love thing? The people I cared about seemed to drift away eventually, and it was hard to believe that they would ever stay. If I was honest I'd always had this fear that Phil would go.

Jack wanted me so much and claimed he hadn't been near a woman for a long time. I could feel his loneliness which was all wrapped up in carnal desire, to have a woman again after so much time alone. That had an intoxicating effect on me and the sadness disappeared. I just wanted him.

Benji was interrupting us and Jack got irritated. I could tell he was wondering why this passionate encounter had to be spoilt by a dog. He seemed extremely irritated now which was curbing my desire. I thought, no I knew, that he wanted us to go upstairs, but he didn't like to ask, and I didn't want to suggest it, for some stupid school-girlish reason of not wanting to appear too forward.

Finally, we both stood up and went upstairs holding hands. I wanted it to be over because I felt so nervous. I slipped into bed feeling like a young girl, and he moved on top of me quickly. It was like the first time, like being a virgin when you'd only slept with one man for twenty years. Madonna's words ran

Brown Eyes

through my head, and I felt like singing, 'Like a virgin... for the very first time.' That would have been extremely inappropriate!

It felt strange that he wasn't Phil and I kept noticing details, like a spot on his back, the hair on his chest, everything seemed different. And before I could think much more it was all over, and I lay there feeling consumed with guilt - guilty that I'd enjoyed it so much that I wanted to do it again and again. And what would my mother say? And Tania? And the kids? Why did I have to think of them?

Guilty that I'd enjoyed it so much with someone new and wanting it to happen again, right then. It was like I'd fallen in love with him, and I felt sexy and young, and guilty and embarrassed all at the same time.

'I've been dreaming of this for several weeks now,' he said.

Did I want all this involvement? Wasn't it easier to be alone now, not to get involved and have all that hurt again and what about the kids? How would they take it?

The next time we made love it was slower and afterwards he dressed, and I put on a dressing gown, and we went downstairs and had croissants and coffee together. I kept thinking about the sex, and wanting to do it again, but would he think I was too keen? It was too difficult to analyse, but there was so much that came into play – I was lonely, heartbroken, desperate for love, and above all

Brown Eyes

I wanted to pay Phil back. Now I was doing something that he wouldn't like, and it felt mighty good.

He kissed me hard on the mouth as if he were saying goodbye and I felt such a surge of desire that when he held me near, I was like putty in his hands.

Benji was safely shut away in the kitchen, no doubt with his ears pricked up. We embraced for several minutes and, he said huskily,

'Have you got time?'

Unable to speak I just nodded so we went upstairs quickly but silently. This time it was even more slow and loving and I felt completely at ease in his arms. I even managed to cope with the way he looked into my eyes, something I was not normally comfortable with − not that it'd happened for a long time.

I felt waves of love and excitement sweeping over me. This was better than ever before, better than Phil and it transported me back to that time years and years ago when this sort of thing happened more often. I used to fall in love so easily and believed that he was 'the one' and now I felt like it again.

Time was moving fast, and finally he got out of bed, kissed me quickly and dashed off to pick up his son.

'I'll ring you tomorrow,' he called from the bottom of the stairs, and I believed him.

Brown Eyes

I got showered hurriedly and went downstairs to take Benji out. He appeared to be sulking, but I sat down with him and told him,

'I've had the most fantastic experience and I feel like I'm in love. I know it's silly.' Of course, he didn't know what I was saying.

Brown Eyes

Benji

I didn't want her to think I was cross with her, but what an insult. Did they think I could be fobbed off like this? I didn't want this man coming into our lives disrupting everything for everyone. I wanted Phil to come back and Meriel to come to her senses and ask him to move back in. If this chap got his way everything would change and what about the children? Didn't they get any say?

She sat by me and stroked me, and I felt so miserable even though I tried to give her my full attention. I didn't like the sound of what she was saying at all. Surely, she couldn't just forget all about Phil and have this other man in his place, as if husbands were totally dispensable?

They're worse than dogs, these humans. Some dogs are not at all discerning and they move from partner to partner but I'm not like that. Some dogs just wanted what they can get from each other and their owners. I'd be happy to be with Rosie, the most gorgeous boxer I've ever known. There was no point in dreaming, I'd got to think of a plan to keep this family together.

13

Meriel

It was another three weeks before I got to see Jack again. He was much more available than me, and one thing and another prevented me from seeing him on his own for a date.

I'd not known passion like this for years, if ever, and I just wanted it to last forever. He gave me a hard time about not being available for him for the last few weeks but what could I do? But when he was caressing me, I just wanted to be with him all the time.

I couldn't remember ever thinking about sex this much in my life. It was all the time and I wanted it all the time. I thought about sex when I was on the bus, in the supermarket, in business meetings. What was happening to me? Here I was at forty-six and most of my friends were telling me how they couldn't be bothered any more.

'I'm sorry Jack but it's nine o'clock. I really must go. I've got to pick up Rick and take him to a football match.'

'Why can't Phil do it?' he asked.

'He's doing something else.'

Brown Eyes

'Why?'

Oh God does he have to keep questioning me?

'Because, Jack. I don't want to have to explain everything.'

He tried to pull me back and I wanted to, but it just wasn't right to be late for Rick.

'I must go.'

Jack kept phoning me and asking me out all the time. It sounded like I was making a lot of lame excuses, but now I am a single parent and there is plenty for me to organise. Some nights I had to be in two places at once and Phil wasn't being very helpful.

'I do want to be with you, Jack but I've got two teenage children. You know what it's like, you've got kids.'

'Sort of.'

I wondered how much he did understand. Perhaps he hadn't done much for his children.

'I really enjoyed last weekend but I can't wait to see you again.'

'You'll just have to. We'll have a great time – it can be worth waiting for.'

'It had better be.'

I was feeling pressurised. Was it fair that he kept on at me like this? My children come first but I also wanted this relationship because I liked him and at times I felt as if I loved him. Could I just be on the rebound?

Brown Eyes

I still felt a real buzz when I thought about him. I didn't want him to spoil this, because I was very keen, as long as he didn't ruin it for me.

That night at about 11 the doorbell rang, and it was him. My first feeling was one of annoyance that he should come round unannounced when the kids were in. But I gave in quickly because the electricity between us left me feeling out of control. I just couldn't resist him. What was it about this man? In some ways he wasn't that attractive, and he wasn't really my type but he had such a strong effect on me.

'I need to see you,' he said as he walked in.

'Is there a problem?'

'Not really. It's just I can't bear being without you. I've fallen in love with you Meriel and I just need you all the time. I want you so much.'

I felt flattered but shocked. It was only a month now and he had said that he'd fallen in love with me. Where did that leave me? I couldn't say the same. He put his arms round me and pulled me near and started kissing me.

Benji started to growl.

'Put that dog out of the room please Meriel.'

I shut Benji in the kitchen. Turning back, I asked,

Brown Eyes

'Do you want a drink? A coffee?'

'No. Just come here.'

He was clearly feeling very passionate, but I was well aware that my children were in the house, and Benji had decided to be a complete pain and was scratching at the door and whining loudly.

'I can't, not here.'

'Well upstairs then. I can't wait.'

My body was succumbing even if my mind was trying hard to hang on.

'You'll have to leave after.'

'Why? Why can't you let your children know that I'm around to stay?'

'I'm not ready for that. They're not ready.'

'Meriel please. I just want you.'

Against my better judgement I took him upstairs, petrified that one of the kids would see him. I locked my door so that they wouldn't suddenly burst in. I put the radio on softly.

As soon as he touched me, I felt my body turn to jelly and I wanted him desperately too. Why was it that someone could make me feel so passionate that I am was confused about how I felt for him and for Phil, whom I thought I still loved?

14

Benji

Meriel seemed to have so much work to do she could barely think straight, and I'd heard her say that she was doing some research for a new TV series on immigrants living in London. She seemed odd to me, not how she normally is. That Jack fellow seemed to have a strange effect on her, as if she was going mad.

Despite being so upset some of the time, when she spoke to work people, she sounded completely normal. I can't imagine how – if I am upset the only thing that cheers me up is a good walk, a cuddle with my owners, a good bone, or Rosie!

I heard Meriel pick up the phone cursing to herself,

'I'm so busy. I can't take any time now.'

Then her face dropped, and she looked as if she were going to cry. Oh no not again.

'Cathy, oh I'm so sorry. I'll come round.'

She shoved me – yes that's what it felt like – in the boot and drove off far too fast, so I was falling over in the boot as she sped round

Brown Eyes

corners. I had no idea what was going on, but she was really tense and seemed to be crying.

We arrived at Cathy's and she hugged her without letting me out of the car. They held on to each other for ages. What on earth was going on?

Phil had moved out and she seemed to have lost interest in him – it was all Jack from the park and you know how I felt about him. The kids were as bad as ever but probably worse because they were hurting, and she just didn't know how to deal with them. And I've heard her telling Tania that her work was a mess because she had a new boss who had obsessive compulsive something, whatever that is, and expected her to have it as well.

Meriel

This loneliness was present all the time in the pit of my stomach and in my throat. I just couldn't help wondering at the fact that when Phil lived with me, I was either irritated or just fed up with him. And now he was no longer there, this desperate loneliness was taking me over.

I only felt OK when I was sitting down with the children or talking to one of my friends like Tania or Cathy, or when Jack and I were ensconced. And somehow this loneliness felt as if it was coming from deep

Brown Eyes

inside and way back in my life because I'd felt it before but I'm not sure when.

Perhaps it was when I was a child and Mum and Dad went away and left me with a friend of the family with whom I had no rapport at all. In fact, I was left with the child of the friend of the family and their cleaner, who was nice. I had no relationship with this child though, and felt bereft that my parents had left me.

This was when they used to get on, before my dad moved on to newer pastures. But no thought was given to me and how I'd feel being dumped off at the age of eight.

I had never talked about this loneliness because it felt like a weakness, and I didn't want to start crying and feel stupid. Perhaps other people felt like this too, but they never said so. It was so much easier to have an object for unhappiness like a mean husband, an unfaithful husband or someone who was just there to be blamed – well I did now. But loneliness wasn't like that – it came from deep inside.

As I drove up to Cathy's I was wondering if life could get any worse. And it did. Tania's car was already there when I walked in, and Cathy looked awfully pale.

'Are you OK?' I asked.

'Sit down and I'll get you a chamomile tea.'

Brown Eyes

I noticed she didn't ask me what I wanted, but decided for me, but that wasn't important, just strange. Something was very wrong.

Tania and I were quiet, looking at Cathy in dreaded anticipation. My stomach was literally turning over and felt painful.

'It's come back.'

We both gasped – we knew what she meant.

'How do you know?'

'I felt it and so I went to the hospital, and they said there's another tumour in the same breast but it's much worse than the other one.'

'Oh no. I don't believe it.'

Things could definitely get worse. Cathy's wonderful optimistic nature, that had given her complete belief that life would just turn out brilliantly for all of us, was completely dashed now. It was all going wrong. And was Cathy going to be able to fight it?

'What's the prognosis?'

'It's not so good. They'll probably remove the lump or the whole breast but if it's spread it could have gone elsewhere.'

'Can they tell you?'

'Yes, but are they always right? I don't know.'

'I'll do anything I can to help you get through this,' I mumbled. It was rushing through my mind. I mustn't be dramatic; I

Brown Eyes

mustn't assume she's not going to live. I had to be positive, but realistic, I didn't want her to think I felt sorry for her, but I was there for her. Oh, it was so difficult. And I might have had problems in my marriage and all that goes with it, but at least I was not facing this.

Cathy smiled.

'I know. I know I've got the two best friends anyone could ever have.'

'How's Andy taking it?'

'Well, you know Andy. He always expects everything to be fine because he seems to think it will sort itself out. He might be in for a shock.'

'Shall we sit outside and Benji can play in the garden?'

Benji

I didn't feel like playing at all. I wanted to hear, to know what the problem was. I wandered off and did a few wees, came back and looked at them.

'It's as if he knows,' Meriel said, touching me lightly with her hand.

Cathy was crying.

'I can't believe this has happened. I've tried so hard and been so good and it's come back.'

'I know. We just have to be really strong. I'm sure you can succeed again.'

Brown Eyes

'I'm not, Meriel. This is not good, when cancer comes back you've had it.'

She started to sob and Meriel sat with her arms around her. She didn't seem to know what to say but she looked as if she really loved her, and I didn't even feel jealous. I didn't know what cancer is but this seemed to be very serious.

Meriel

I was living with a sense of dread all the time and it's not to do with Phil. I woke up in the morning and thought about Cathy. I went to bed at night and Cathy was on my mind. I woke up in the night and she was there again. I lay awake worrying that she was awake and frightened. What must it feel like to know that your days were numbered and that you've got two children who you wouldn't see grow up?

And then I had waves of hope – she'd be all right, I knew she would. She could fight this. She'd been going for five years, she had been living a normal life, so healthy. But was I just kidding myself like I did in the past, to my detriment? Maybe she wouldn't make it.

Right now, I needed to be there for her, and at times I just wanted to shrink away from it all. She was getting incredibly thin and I knew it was not good. Cathy still rushed

Brown Eyes

around trying to do as much as she could in a normal way and not frighten the kids. But even though she looked so thin her face was just glowing and beautiful. I kept wondering if it was some strange phenomenon that happened at the end of life. After all, she was still only forty-eight. It was as if all the healthy eating had made her look so well, and yet she was dying now, and it was imminent.

Somehow, I just did not believe that she was going to die. Deep inside me was a belief that she would kick this cancer, but I'd had this feeling in the past, and been wrong.

Much as I wanted to run away, I had to do the opposite. She absolutely relied on me to be there for her, to be on the phone, to go and see her and to be a rock for her when she was falling apart. I could do this, but inside I was crippled with pain. When I got out of her house I couldn't stop crying, but when I was there I managed to be encouraging and tried to say the right thing.

One day I was sitting with her and she started to cry.

'I've been thinking about my funeral,' she said.

She lifted her hand to her face and clenched her fist which she wept into. I got up and went and sit next to her on the garden seat. Never in my life had I sat with someone who was crying about the fact that they were going to die. And still I said,

Brown Eyes

'No, I'm just sure it is going to be OK. I have such a strong feeling.'

'Isn't it just,' she asked me, 'that you don't want to have a friend die?'

'I know what you mean. I just can't and don't believe it,' I say, knowing that perhaps I really was kidding myself, but not her.

And it's true I couldn't cope with a friend dying so I was in denial, and I wanted so much to be right.

We got side-tracked and didn't talk about her funeral, and I regretted it. This was perhaps the only time that she was going to talk it through, and I didn't encourage it. I left her feeling terrible, and again I was in tears all the way home. As I was driving up a road near home I had to pull over because a large car was pushing me into the side, and it was just my luck that I scraped my car on a telegraph pole which was concealed in the hedge.

I arrived at Tania's and burst into tears straightaway.

'She's going to die. Cathy's going to die.'

'Now, now,' Tania said, putting her arms right around me and hugging me close.

'You must be positive, she's fine. She will be fine.'

'Tania, I can assure you she isn't fine. She is going to die. I've only just realised. I've been kidding myself and now I know I can't

Brown Eyes

do it any longer. She's a shadow of herself. Her body is so thin and frail, all she can do is sit in the garden and eat the food her mother brings her. She doesn't worry about the vegan diet anymore, she just eats what her mother gives her and that includes bread, butter, meat, anything. Why should she be so strict now? She just eats what she wants and her mother knows that she's going to die, so she makes it for her.'

Tania looked really worried now, and she dissolves into tears.

'What are we going to do, Meriel?'

'Nothing, we can't do anything, except to be there for her.'

From that day on, I went every day. Even when her mother said she didn't want to see anyone anymore, I still went up and saw her. She did want to see me, but I wasn't to wear her out. I talked to her and she slept. I sat beside her and held her hand and I had the strangest feeling. A surge of energy flowed through my body and into my hands, and when I told her, she said so quietly,

'I know. I felt it.'

'I never felt it would come to this,' Cathy told me.

'I find it so hard to believe. I never believed it at all. And I still don't'

She looked at me and she was the one in charge. She knew I was wrong and that I could not accept it. But she fully accepted now

Brown Eyes

that she was not going to be here much longer, not even a week. And so, I too had to accept it.

She got up to go to the loo. She staggered there, her thin little legs struggling to hold her up. I tidied the bed so that it would be more comfortable when she got back.

'Sorry Meriel, I'm so tired. I must sleep.'

'I'll leave you now.'

Tears dropped down our faces. We knew it was the last time we'd see each other.

'You've been a good friend to me,' she said.

'You have been a good friend to me too.'

'Try to forgive Phil. You love each other.'

They were her last words. She was too tired, too faded to cry, but I couldn't stop the tears from coming.

'I'm sorry,' I apologised. 'I can't help it.'

She just looked at me. What was she thinking? Now she was about to die and she was only forty-eight.

I smiled at her and I felt joyful and loving towards her, and I told her. I kissed her hair and left her.

Downstairs I saw Andy but we didn't speak. We just hugged. We knew what was coming.

Ricky took the call and came over to hand me the phone. He knew what it was about. I spoke to Andy.

Brown Eyes

'She died just now in my arms,' he told me. I could hardly speak, but I managed,

'Thank you.'

He said, 'You can come over if you like.'

I put down the phone and burst into tears and my lovely son put his arm around me and I put my head on his shoulder and cried. This was a complete reversal of roles.

Three hours later I rang Andy.

'Is it OK to come?'

In the hallway I met Cathy's mother and her son, Jamie.

'Would you like to go and see her?' Daphne asked me.

'Yes,' I said, knowing I wanted to do this, even though I'd never been brave enough before.

We went upstairs and into her bedroom where everything looked as it always did, but she was lying there with her mouth open. There were four of us in the room. Her mother, her sister, her son and me. We all stood in a row holding hands with each other, and it was surreal. We talked a little bit, about what I couldn't remember. It seemed so strange. She was lying there but she was no longer with us.

Benji

Brown Eyes

I never knew anything about dying before, apart from dead mice that the cat brought in. All I knew now was that Meriel was deeply despairing and cried a lot and I tried to comfort her, to put my paw on her and to be there for her to cry on. I sometimes whined to show how much I cared for her. She was devastated.

You could have thought that because she was grieving so much Meriel would have ignored me, but it was the complete opposite. I was the one she turned to and said how she felt – of course, she didn't know that I understood as much as I did.

Often she would lean over me and hug me and cry. I cried as well but tried not to make any noise. It's really hard to see your owner in so much pain. And she used to say to me,

'I miss her so much. I never thought this would happen. Don't ever go Benji.'

This was difficult for me because I knew that she'd lost her pet dog when she was a child. I don't mean that she was careless and couldn't find them but they died, and she told her friend Tania that she had been completely heartbroken. I never want to leave her, but I have heard that we don't have such a long life as humans and therefore I'm bound to let her down.

Day after day we walked to the same spot where she sat on the bench in the park overlooking Cathy's back garden. Meriel

Brown Eyes

would close her eyes and tilt her face up to the sky, as if she was looking at the heavens in the hope that she would commune with Cathy.

I tried to act very sensibly when she did this because I knew it was a special time. I sat down beside her and waited for her. I could just feel how much this time meant to her and for that reason it became very special to me too. Even when some really fun dogs were playing on the grass I stayed sitting and didn't pull on my lead for fear of disturbing her.

I couldn't count in time terms but sometimes this would go on for a long time and afterwards she would have tears running down her face, but it always made her feel better. I felt privileged to be there experiencing this with her.

Meriel went to see Tania lots of times. They were grieving together and sometimes they cried and hugged each other, and I felt very jealous and whined a bit, but I knew that Tania was helping Meriel and as I loved her so much, I wanted her to help.

Meriel

'I've never cried so much as I have this year. I keep thinking there can't be any more tears, but they keep on coming.'

'It's good to get it out, isn't it? Just think of poor Cathy and how she didn't really cry

Brown Eyes

enough. How brave she was and how she carried this thing all on her own,' Tania said.

'She did really. I suppose that's what you do when you have a terminal illness. No one can do it for you, however much they love you.'

'I just hope that we were able to support her as much as we possibly could.'

'It was a great comfort to her. More than at any time of her life she knew that she was so loved by people, that she died in that knowledge, which is how it should be and often isn't.'

'Rarely is. She had real closure with so many people, and that's incredibly important but how can you have that if you die suddenly? A friend of Jake's father died suddenly last week. In fact, Jake was round there, and I picked him up and spoke to the dad on the Sunday and the next evening he was dead from a heart attack. He was only forty-nine.'

'That's awful. What a shock for everyone. Yes, it's true you can't have closure in that situation, can you?'

'Life seems to be getting more and more difficult. We've both suffered a great loss, you and Phil have split up and need I start on about my problems?'

Tania was definitely finding it difficult being a single parent with three teenagers and although she had the solace of her young

Brown Eyes

lover, she had the hassle of Dave who hadn't taken kindly to the split, and he seemed wholly reluctant to pay towards the kids' upkeep. Money was a constant problem for Tania and although a well-qualified teacher she just couldn't make ends meet.

Yet, Tania was happy in many other ways.

'I'm following my heart and that's more important than anything.'

'You know I'm finding that I'm more peaceful and calm since Cathy died,' I told her. 'All my anger has evaporated.'

'That's good. I know what you mean. Dave has upset the children again and I'm just thinking, so what?'

'You have so much to put up with that man. What's he done now?'

'He asked them all over last weekend and you know how much Dan hates going, but he went. Apparently, Joanna told me he was saying that I was a bitch and that all I wanted to do was grab money off him. Can you believe it?'

'Just do what's right Tania. They are his children and he isn't supporting them at all. He's punishing them because of you, which seems very unfair. All you can do is try your hardest to be happy yourself, so that you do right by the children. I'm a fine one to speak after how I treat mine, but neither of us would want to be without them.'

Brown Eyes

'No of course not. But at this age they aren't very rewarding. Dan grunts at me most of the time, Joanna has tantrums and even Jake is still very difficult. He's so incredibly selfish and I wonder what I've done to deserve it.'

'They'll adore you one day, when they grow up.'

'But when? Don't they all stay at home much longer these days?'

'It does seem that way. So many of them are so spoilt - money's usually laid on a plate – sorry it's not in your case.'

'But what Dave does is when they go over, he gives them about £100 each which is about time, but of course Dan just squanders it on computer games and then tells me he's got no money.'

'It's tough Tania. Just hang in there. You're normally the one giving me advice.'

'You know what, Meriel. I'm great at advice to other people, but when it's me I'm not so good.'

'I admire you for what you do. You've got your life more together than me. At least you got that man out of your bed and have the freedom to get on with your life.'

'And so have you.'

'Yes, I have. But I've realised I don't want him out of my life.'

'Good.'

Brown Eyes

'Good? What do you mean?'

'You've recognised what was obvious all along.'

'Was it?'

'I think so, certainly to Cathy and me. You love the guy – you were just angry with him. Don't you think it had something to do with your mother?'

'What do you mean? I suppose, you could be right. I was wondering about that yesterday.'

'What are you going to do?'

'I think it's too late.'

'Never too late.'

'But he's seeing that girl.'

'Didn't he tell you that she meant nothing?'

'That's very easy to say when you're screwing someone.'

'I know it's not easy for you, but what have you got to lose? You need to tell him, Meriel. This is your life and if you stay split up forever when you love him, what's the point? He's told you he loves you.'

'Yes, but all we do is argue when we meet. I don't know what to do.'

'You do.'

'And can he offer what I need? Oh I don't know. I'm all involved with Jack now too. And I don't know what I'm doing or why I'm doing it. I just want to be looked after I

Brown Eyes

suppose, and when I'm with Jack I am completely taken over with, I don't know what. I just seem to be helpless, but I do enjoy it.'

We laughed, and it felt so good.

'Meriel. I never thought you'd got it in you. Good for you.'

'And it feels good to know that Phil probably wouldn't like it.'

'Is this all about revenge then?'

'Yeah, partly, but there's a fair amount of pleasure.'

I laughed again and hugged her.

'It's good to laugh when we are so taken over by it all – Cathy I mean. I love having you to talk to, and that's one of the things I miss so much about Cath – she was so sympathetic, so caring and I knew, I just knew that she'd listen to me. Not stand in the doorway looking at her watch and saying, 'I've really got to get on.'

'Of course, sometimes she was busy, but she was a listening, caring ear and that's what we love so much about each other.'

Tania just nodded and smiled.

'We went for a drink with some of Paul's friends last night for the first time.'

'How was it?'

'Well quite honestly. I felt like an old mother because they were just like Danny – so immature. They could have been my sons and

Brown Eyes

to be honest Paul drank quite a lot and I've never known him like that. He was quite stupid.'

'In what way?'

'Just banal – the kind of jokes he made and the things he said. I just felt like I shouldn't have been there.'

'Did he know you felt uncomfortable?'

'He's quite sensitive. After a while he took me back to his place and then, of course, you can imagine I forgot all about it. He's just such an adept lover that I can't give him up.'

'Why should you?'

'Yes, why should I? I'm only married in name and it's time I had some fun. I just won't go out with his friends again. I imagine myself giving them advice – you know the older woman giving them the benefits of my long life.'

'Not that long!'

I had got used to Tania looking sexy, slim and full of life these days, but I'm still not sure that she's as in love with Paul as she says. I'm finding with Jack that a lot of it is lust and not love, but it's incredibly easy to mix them up with each other. At first, I thought I loved Jack because it was simply euphoric.

'Maybe not! It just makes you realise that you think you know someone, love them even, but you don't know them at all.'

'And do you love him?'

Brown Eyes

'Not really. It's just so bloody flattering having a young guy like him fancying me and making me feel so good. He makes me feel as if I'm a young sexual woman and I love it. Dave never ever made me feel like that. All I felt with him was that he wanted to get it over with, so he'd get his oats but nothing romantic.'

'Not even in the early days?'

'We all overlook everything in the early days. And to be honest I was so keen to have children and be a wife that I just settled for second best. I wouldn't do it again. I'm not even sure I want to live with a man now.'

'Just sleep with one.'

'Yes! I don't want to stop seeing Paul. But I'm not in love with him.'

'Or Dave.'

'No. I absolutely know I don't love him now, if I ever did. Perhaps I was in love with the idea of the security and the lifestyle he used to give me. I must stress the 'used to' because nowadays he doesn't provide anything. But he's not in demand in the workplace like he used to be.'

'The trouble with advertising is it's a young business and once you're near to fifty you're considered far too old.'

'Yes, and he hasn't really been that smart about keeping up his contacts. I couldn't tell him because he always knew better. I won't get much when we split it all up.'

Brown Eyes

'Just half of everything you own.'

'If he hasn't remortgaged it to the hilt.'

'Has he?'

'I'm not entirely sure.'

'You must be entitled to check.'

'I'll look into it. I just hope he supports them through uni.'

15

Meriel

It was a rare late summer day in September when the sun was constant. It felt like another country. I noticed the temperature in the car was on 25 even at 4 o'clock in the afternoon.

As I drove along, I was thinking about what to cook for supper when I realised it was too dark for sunglasses. The sky had darkened very quickly, and the forecast rain was on its way.

By the time I got home spots of rain were coming through the sunroof of the car, but I didn't want to close it because it was still sweltering. As I took the shopping inside the heavens opened. I ran upstairs and closed the windows. It came down in torrents. This was no longer like English rain – it had turned sub-tropical and only a few days earlier there had been hailstones the size of marbles.

Then as quickly as it had arrived, the rain cleared away and the sky was a mixed colour, bright in the north and dark in the south as the clouds moved down the coast. It was dry enough to take Benji out now, so I put on a

Brown Eyes

pair of Wellington boots and set off down the road to the field that had the view of the sea.

The field sloped down one side of the hill and up the other. Benji loved it because it was full of long grass and plenty of smells. He bounded along with his ears flopping up and down.

It was a strange evening; unlike any I'd ever experienced here before. The heat from the land and the volume of rain had combined to create a patchy mist coming up from the ground. The sea in the distance was so misty I could hardly see it.

As dusk fell it gave an eerie feel to the area, but at the same time a peaceful, silent atmosphere. Only Benji and I were in the field.

I stood still and drank in the atmosphere and Benji stopped and sat quietly beside me. It was always out in the open in nature that I sensed my lost friend, in a way that I had never experienced before – not with my father or my gran whom I'd been so close to.

I felt at peace for the first time in years, or could it be in my entire life? Cathy's death had brought me to this point in my life where I experienced a kind of acceptance and a loss of fear about my own immortality, something I had never been able to cope with before.

I saw moving low across the long grass something brown and large. I looked carefully – in this light I could be imagining it, but it

Brown Eyes

was a huge bird. Maybe a falcon but I didn't know if it was. Its wings spanned several feet and it was swooping low over the grasses.

The countryside here was rich with wildlife and only three months earlier when I was walking with Cathy, I had seen some animals in the woods hopping like kangaroos but with white bobtails. I thought I was imagining it – they were much too big to be rabbits, and kangaroos in England - really? It was later when we saw a man walking in the woods and asked him that he explained that they were baby deer.

'With white bobtails?'

'Yes,' he said. 'They have them – just like rabbits.'

I stopped again. That time I'd been here with Cathy seemed so recent and now she was gone – thank goodness I had spent time with her talking so closely and being supportive, and vice-versa. Previous disagreements were all forgotten by then and we thoroughly enjoyed each other's company.

Losing Cathy had been one of the biggest shocks of my life and at times I felt I would never get over it. It wasn't what anyone expected, to lose a friend who was younger and still in her prime. But I was coping with it and I would get over it and never forget her.

It made me realise how much I loved my friends, my family and Phil. I loved Phil in my heart but I've been so angry with him for

Brown Eyes

having an affair, for betraying me just like my father had done to my mother.

Losing Cathy had made me realise how devastated I would be if it were Phil, the man I'd had children with, whom I'd shared my life with for twenty years. Why was I doing this? Was all the anger to do with my mother and completely misplaced on Phil? And perhaps it was time to forgive my mother too. She was seventy-eight now and she wasn't going to be there forever. What was the point of that either?

I was disappointed in myself but due to so much going on, I was very aware that I'd changed irrevocably. In future, I am sure I would be less judgemental of people.

I wasn't to know what kind of relationship my parents had. My father had been quite a cool customer – it must have been hard for Mum.

The thought struck me. Perhaps Phil was looking for love – consolation for a wife who still held back all the time and couldn't let her emotions flow. He was such a loving man and I'd rebuffed him, turned away his advances and eventually he'd found someone else. And I was the cause.

Tania would say,

'Don't beat yourself up Meriel.'

I was old enough to know that going round blaming yourself for the rest of your life was

Brown Eyes

not the answer. I had to move on and I knew
in my heart that now was the time I would.

16

Benji

The sun had been shining all day and it suddenly started raining. I heard Meriel saying to the kids,

'It's raining cats and dogs.'

What ever could she mean? I could only see water.

I was getting bored because she'd been on the talking thing to Tania for a very long time. It was loud so I could hear what Tania was saying as well.

I was beginning to hear that Meriel wasn't so keen on Jack anymore. He was becoming a pain in the neck to her, and no one was more pleased than me. He was really irritating me. He kept ringing her up, turning up at inappropriate times uninvited, and moaning and moaning about her not being available.

'He's just on the phone all the time, asking to see me,' she told Tania. 'I feel as if he's trying to control me, it's just too heavy for words. In a way I'm a free agent now, but he's trying to tie me down.'

Brown Eyes

'I know it's nice but I feel like he's desperate and that's so off -putting. And gradually after not being able to keep my hands off him, he is becoming less and less attractive and I wonder what I saw in him. I've never really liked men with his sort of looks, and I know you'd say that's not important, but I wonder what was I thinking of?'

'That's because you still love Phil.'

'Oh stop it, Tania. It's too late now. That's over.'

I felt so deflated when she said that. I put my head down on my paws and closed my eyes.

'It isn't over. Why should it be? If two people want to be together they can be. There's nothing stopping you and neither of you has made any commitment, have you?'

'Well, no, I haven't anyway. I just feel sorry for Jack after all the promises I gave him.'

'That's life Meriel. We all do it. They do it to us.'

'But he didn't ask for this, did he?'

'I'm afraid that anyone who gets involved asks for it. It's the risk you take, and if no one took any risks we'd never love anyone would we?'

'What am I going to do Tania?'

'Maybe you should sort out Jack first.'

Brown Eyes

'What tell him I'm a heartless bitch, and I'm not interested after all?'

I couldn't understand why she compared herself to a female dog at all.

'Pretty much... No,' Tania laughed. 'Say that your marriage isn't over. Just tell him the truth. What more can you do? That's the fairest kindest way to deal with it – it is the truth, isn't it?'

'Yes.'

I couldn't help it but my tail seemed to know things before I did and was twitching and then moving and scraping the ground. I sprang up and gave it full rein.

'You'd think Benji understood. He leapt up and wagged his tail.'

They made that laughing noise.

'See he wants you to get back together, doesn't he?' Tania said.

I wish I could speak.

'Probably – he loves Phil. But the thing is, we're forgetting about Laura. I saw him with her.'

'When?'

'He came to the door and she was in the car. I was heartbroken. I sort of knew then.'

'Oh God! You two. If it's not one it's the other. All you can do is tell him how you feel.'

'What, when he's seeing her? How can I?'

'Don't you think she's just someone to pass the time with? He'd far rather be with you but

Brown Eyes

as far as he's concerned, you're involved with Jack and maybe he thinks it's too late. If you don't say something how's he ever going to know?'

'I suppose this happens all the time, doesn't it? But you can't just slot in where you left off? Everything's changed.'

'And that's good. You needed everything to change. There's no doubt that you will have to work on it – that's the only way these things can become better.'

I've no idea what this work is that they have to do. Perhaps in the garden or the house, but it all sounds positive. Meriel called me out into the car. I jumped into the boot quickly and as we drove through town she had a happy face, a joyous thing to behold.

When we got back home Elly and Rick were back.

'What's the matter darling – why are you crying? Has someone upset you at school?' Meriel was talking to Elly.

This is a bit dumb. Her dad's left, that's why she's upset.

'No.'

'Well, what is it?'

'I can't say.'

'It's easier if you do and then maybe I can help.'

'That's just it, you can't help. You can't do anything.'

Brown Eyes

'Why?'

'Because it's about Dad.'

'Oh. I suppose I can't.'

'I just am so scared that he's going to forget all about me. And Rick too. Because I heard, someone told me that about a fifth of dads lose touch with their children.'

Meriel looked upset and angry.

'He won't. He does love you. Whatever our problems are he won't leave you. Talk to him.'

'I can't.'

'Why?'

'He's not easy to talk to.'

'I suppose that's true and if you can get him when he's not with her.'

I didn't even want to hear this. I'd never treat a puppy like this. Meriel, much as I love her, should put Elly first. It seemed so mean to be angry like this – couldn't she see what it's doing? And besides she could have Phil back if only she'd forget this stupid pride.

Ricky crept into the hall and was listening to the conversation, but he didn't join in. He didn't say anything much to anyone, except me. Because I was looking at him Meriel looked up,

'Rick? Is that you? Look at the state of your hair.'

He grunted and went upstairs and then at the top of the stairs he called me,

Brown Eyes

'Benji, come on.'

I'm not really allowed in the bedrooms, but the discussion was upsetting me. So I jumped up the stairs two at a time and Meriel didn't even say a word.

Mind you I wished I hadn't come into his room because Ricky's way of dealing with things is rather violent. He started chucking stuff around the room and swearing and I was terrified he was going to hit me with a ball or something. I managed to squeeze under the bed. Why did he call me up here if he was going to throw things around?

And was this because of what he'd heard? These kids were really suffering and neither parent seemed to be aware of it really. Meriel had shut up Elly by what she said, and so now she wouldn't tell her mum any more.

The throwing stopped and I was standing by the door, waiting to go out. He came crawling up like another dog and hung on to me, wanting to play. I just didn't know what to do, he might have got violent again.

Then he let me out because I was whining and when I got downstairs, I could hear Meriel and Elly having a kind of argument.

'Who says this happens all the time anyway?'

'A girl at school told me.'

'Who was that? That's not very tactful.'

'If it's true I ought to be told.'

Brown Eyes

'It's a statistic but everyone's individual and I'm sure that's not in Dad's mind, but then how do I know what's in his mind?'

Elly's face dropped – that was no consolation for her. Meriel gave out mixed messages all the time.

17

Benji

I heard Meriel's conversation with Tania, and was so delighted that everything would be normal again, but it hasn't been. Meriel didn't even contact Phil to say what she was thinking, and she had that Jack bloke round again and he went upstairs with her. I didn't know what they do upstairs, but I wasn't sure if they were going to have puppies now, well children anyway.

They always waited for the children to be away. I hated this bloke and I'd even thought of biting his ankles. He was totally getting in the way of our future happiness and I can't stand it.

I heard her on the phone to Tania and she was saying,

'Not yet. Yes, I will but I'm scared.'

What had anyone got to do to make her realise?

'Mum.' Elly appeared in the room. 'You know Laura.'

'Not exactly dear.'

Brown Eyes

'Well you know who I mean. Actually, I thought she was quite cool.'

Meriel winced and I whimpered despite myself.

'Thanks Elly,' Meriel said a bit sarcastically. And Elly didn't get it and carried on.

'She wore these fantastic clothes and she's got those really long nails – you know.'

'Actually Elly. I don't know and I really don't want to. She's your dad's,' she seemed to struggle for a word, 'Well, girlfriend, and I don't want to know much about her even if she is cool.'

'You've got that bloke.'

'His name's Jack.'

'Well you're seeing him, so why shouldn't Dad?'

'I didn't say he shouldn't. It's just that I don't want to know about her. OK? I don't want to know what he does or who he's with or what she's like, OK?'

She was getting really ratty now.

'Well I can tell you that,' Elly said in a sort of arrogant way.

'He's not seeing her anymore.'

'Really? How do you know?'

'Dad told me.'

'Did he? What did he say?'

'If you really want to know…'

Elly seemed to be enjoying this.

Brown Eyes

'He said that he had stopped seeing Laura because he still loves you.'

I made an involuntary snorting noise, which made Elly laugh and she cuddled me. Meriel smiled and for once they both looked happy.

18

Benji

When Meriel told Tania I must say it was one of the best days of my life.

'It's amazing you know – so much shit or water under the bridge.'

What did she mean?

'And yet you still love each other. Sometimes it's odd this thing with marriage. Some people split up so easily, but for us there's so much more there under the surface and it's only being without him that's made me realise it's there. I do love him, and I can forgive him because what's the point in not doing so?'

'And Jack?'

'I'll have to tell him.'

'It might not just be plain sailing this starting again.'

'No there's a lot to sort out.'

'They're all so blimin' useless, I personally can't see the point of having one let alone two.'

'I haven't got two – I've only got Jack and dare I say it, he's beginning to annoy me.'

Brown Eyes

'Why?' Tania asked in quite a harsh way I thought.

'He keeps on asking me to do this or that, and simpering over me. It's like he's spoiling the relationship. I really enjoyed everything about him, and I mean everything, but it shows it wasn't that deep because now he won't leave me alone, he's pushing me away.'

'Perhaps he's looking for a mummy.'

'He doesn't treat me like one.'

'Only because you're in the first flush of the romance. When he gets his feet under the table he will turn into a little boy and want you to wipe his bottom for him.'

This sounded too disgusting for words. I know that Meriel thinks Tania is too harsh on men and sometimes it annoys her.

'I guess that's it – we all want to have our mummies look after us, because no one gives you such unconditional love. And we get so angry with these men because they treat us as if we are their mothers, but really we want to have someone be our mummy too. That's why it makes us so cross . And because we're women we're so able to mother them, but who does it for us?'

Tania was speaking fast, and I really don't know about what she said. I manage perfectly well without a mummy or a partner. And I'm not at all sure that men are like little boys. I'm sure Phil isn't.

Brown Eyes

'I think we need to learn to understand men, you know, Tania. It's no good women just deciding we're superior – that's behaving like they always did.'

'Except that we are!'

'Well in some ways, but they still have all the power, and there are some decent men out there. They're not all like Dave.'

'Granted. There are one or two, but it is a worry bringing up boys, hoping they won't treat women like Dave has treated me.'

'Perhaps he felt that you hated him?'

'Only because of the way he behaved.'

'Now come on Tania. You'd be the first person to say that we create our own situations. Maybe he felt inferior to you because you're so very capable and you like everything just so. He couldn't match up.'

'Possibly.'

It was true Tania was so fussy that if some hairs dropped off me, she always made a big song and dance about picking them up. I can't help it, but she made me feel as if I were dirty.

I have never seen such a clean house – everything is always in its place, and when you think that she has three kids – and they're usually messier than puppies. I'd heard Meriel telling Phil what a control freak Tania was because she rushed around the whole house tidying every morning and she just made the

Brown Eyes

children's rooms look so perfect that it looked as if they didn't live there.

Meriel sat forward in the chair and looked at Tania.

'It is a great time in history for us women you know. We can leave our husbands because we have the right to do it. Just fifty years ago we wouldn't get any money if we split up with them and look what women had to put up with. They all think they were much happier but there was plenty of unhappiness too. My mum thinks I should just put up with Phil's infidelity but she's a fine one to talk. She may have put up with my dad, but she was just as bad.'

Tania nodded heartily. She'd heard a lot about Meriel's mum, and so had I. When it comes to her mum, I'll defend Meriel to the death.

'Men haven't changed much though, have they?' Meriel continued. 'We have changed radically, not as individuals but as a gender.'

'Try telling that to Afghanistan's women.'

I had no idea what this meant, although I did know an Afghan hound and she seemed to have a nice life.

'There are huge exceptions in the world, but western women have changed enormously and it's good for us because we have greater freedom and we are showing what we can do at last.'

'Instead of being suppressed?'

Brown Eyes

I just couldn't imagine anyone suppressing Tania somehow. In fact, if I could laugh, I would have done. I made a funny sort of crying noise, and they both looked at me.

'It's something we could talk about for hours, but I must go home because Rick and Elly are due in soon.'

Meriel

When he turned up, he was wearing my favourite after-shave and he looked really smart and I felt excited inside, but I hadn't told Jack. I'd made some excuse about Saturday, and I knew it wasn't fair. I simply couldn't face it yet because I was sure he'd give me a hard time.

Going out with Phil was like going on a date with someone new, but with so much history behind us it felt comfortable too. We spent the whole evening discussing the children, my mother, his brother and wife and so it went on and finally Phil said.

'What was it you wanted to say?'

He looked nervous.

'I've been doing some thinking and well.'

I took another sip of Dutch courage.

'I've lost someone recently, someone very close to me.'

Brown Eyes

He nodded – he knew how much Cathy meant to me – why wouldn't he? He cared about her too.

'I don't want to lose someone else.'

I could see he didn't know what I meant.

'You. I don't want to lose you.'

'Really, what's brought this on?'

Perhaps he wasn't going to be very nice.

'When someone dies you realise how much you care about people.'

Somehow, I just couldn't say the love word.

'And you don't want me to die.'

I smiled.

'Of course, I don't but it's more than that. I've realised that if something happened to you, I would lose you forever.'

'So what are you saying Meriel? I'll try not to die if you like.'

'That's not really the point.'

'What is the point?'

'I would like,'

'Yes?'

'Are you still seeing Laura?'

'Is that relevant?'

'Very.'

'No as it happens. I am not seeing her.'

'Why?'

'Because I don't love her. Are you seeing Jack?'

'Yes, I was.'

Brown Eyes

'Well so what's the point of this, if you're putting it about with this builder bloke?'

'Must you put it like that? Anyway, I don't think I want to. I know he's not for me. I just want us to be a family again.'

'Why?'

'Because I've realised that I do love you.'

Phil put down his glass and said,

'Oh.'

And then he reached across the table and held my hand and I started to cry.

'Don't cry. We're in public.'

He always said things like that.

'We'll talk back home.'

He said 'home'.

19

Meriel

Losing a friend at this age was a dreadful shock. Every day I didn't really feel like myself, as if I had changed. I was thinking about her every day, but I was beginning to laugh and smile again. Initially I felt as if I had no confidence and would never be cheerful again. I couldn't feel comfortable in a group of people where I'd always been at ease before.

When someone dies your world is rocked and it's like you have to reset yourself to feel comfortable again – everything you know has gone and you are like a fish out of water.

One day, around six months after her death, I was completely overwhelmed by a yearning to see her again, to talk to her, to phone her, to sit together chatting about all the things we used to discuss.

Cathy was intelligent and knowledgeable, and our conversations ranged from health to politics to minor insecurities and on to relationships all the time. We were very similar and liked to chat at any time so it felt like there was a great hole in my life. We had

Brown Eyes

our ups and downs too as all friendships do, and there were aspects of her life even when she was ill that I felt very critical of, but how was I to know what it felt like to know that you might die?

But with Cathy there were no regrets – I was simply wishing she was here. And the difference between losing a close friend and my dad, was that I didn't share with him the intimacies that I had with Cathy. There were things I told Cathy that I never told anyone else, and that left a big gap in my life.

I miss Cathy's kindness, her caring, her ability to listen no matter what and how, and the fact that she would ring up and just say,

'Hi it's me.'

The yearning was painful because it was completely unable to be fulfilled.

I just couldn't go and see her anymore, but I could conjure her up in my mind or my dreams. I had a lovely dream about her and it felt so real. I'd never quite got to grips with what happened after death, but since Cathy died, I've felt open to anything that meant I might be able to have some sense of her.

As I sat in the garden on a moderately warm spring day I was dreaming about Cathy and patting Benji on the head. He seemed to know when something was wrong and looked at me in an incredibly knowing way as if he could see into my soul. He put his paw on me as if he wanted to protect me from all of this.

Brown Eyes

I kept feeling so lonely, the kind of lonely you can feel in a crowd – just aloneness. I was not physically alone because I had Ricky and Elly to look after, but I feel bereft.

This relationship with Jack was weird and still I hadn't finished it. Mainly because Phil and I never had that chat because the children were still up when we got back after dinner. I was wary of finishing with Jack, and finding out that Phil and Laura were really together, and that he'd lied. I couldn't trust him anymore.

As for Jack, I never thought about him in between our times together, and when I saw him, I wouldn't dream of discussing my innermost thoughts with him. He thought I was so wonderful, but he didn't know me at all.

Mind you, I didn't like talking about how much I missed Cathy with anyone. I only wanted to talk to Cathy so I did, whether she could hear me or not.

What did people do in these situations? I'd had so much shit going on, but I didn't know how to deal with it. The other day I felt like I couldn't breathe – some kind of panic attack. It was all too much to cope with and if Cathy were here, she would have known what to say to me.

Tania said I should go to a counsellor – I'd probably explode. I felt like a minefield and if I started discussing my problems I'd be there

Brown Eyes

for the rest of my life, and how was anyone ever going to really understand?

I was at the supermarket last week and I bumped into Phil's aunt. It was the first time I'd seen her for ages, and we went for a coffee at Starbuck's. I've always liked Jemima but I just didn't know which side of the fence she would be on.

I ordered a latte, and she had a cappuccino. We were talking small talk and suddenly she said,

'Do you miss your friend dear, the one who died?'

'Yes, terribly actually.'

'I know what it's like. I've lost so many people now I can hardly count but it was losing my sister that hurt so much. She was so young – she was only sixty-three.'

'Cathy was just forty-six.'

'I know, it's really tough, isn't it?'

I was biting my lip hard to stay in control and Jemima put a hand on my back. It felt really soothing.

'I can see it hurts.' And that was that. I put my hand over my face and wept.

'I miss her so much and I miss Phil and my life's a mess and… I'm sorry, I'm so sorry.'

'What are you sorry about? It's quite natural to be upset you know. I'll tell you what I've found out in all my long life – that really loneliness isn't to do with other people.

Brown Eyes

It's a feeling inside we can all have and sometimes you can have it when you're with other people but it's you that's making yourself feel lonely.

'I'm not meaning to be harsh. Losing a friend is a huge jolt and I understand, but your happiness will only come from inside, not from Phil or from anyone else.'

While I was blowing my nose I was taking in Jemima. She always looked so neat. Even though she was seventy something, she had such elegance and style. Her grey/blonde hair was twisted neatly up on top of her head with a clip, and she had a smart scarf wound around her neck in a way that never works for me. She was wearing a fabulous jumper with a slimming skirt. As usual she looked immaculate. I had always liked her, but I never knew she was like this, so wise and sympathetic.

'I'm trying to get there, I really am, but I just go round in circles.'

'You need guidance that's why. How are you going to be able to get anywhere unless someone helps you to get there?'

'What do you mean?'

'You need to talk to someone, a professional about this. You know if you feel happier about yourself, I bet he'll come back. I'm sure he loves you anyway.'

'You're right. It's all my insecurities that drove him to this. I've always known that.'

Brown Eyes

And it dawned on me – here I was, ready to throw away a relationship because of my hurt and insecure feelings. How often did people do this?

'But it's too late now.'

'Why?'

'Because I think he's got this Laura,' – I literally spat out her name.

'Has he really, or is she just a diversion?'

'My friend says that.'

'Aren't you seeing someone too?'

'Yes, yes I have been.'

'And do you love him, this new man?'

'NO, of course not.'

'So why can't Phil be doing the same?'

'I hadn't really thought of that.'

'You can love someone else deeply you know even if you are with someone new. Believe me dear I know.'

I wondered what she meant but didn't like to ask. Perhaps old Jemima was a dark horse.

'You mark my words, get that man to counselling and save this relationship. Too many people split up when they shouldn't and all those poor kids.'

My mind drifted to Ricky and Elly. Did they deserve this?

'I'll try,' I said. I felt lighter. 'You've been a tonic for me, thank you. I'm going to go now.'

I kissed Jemima on the cheek. I really wanted to hug her, but we were in Starbuck's

Brown Eyes

and I'd already blubbed all over the place, and besides I didn't do that sort of thing. I picked up my coat. She felt excited but would Phil agree? Hadn't he said that he didn't want someone telling him what to do?

Benji

I was bounding along the road to the car, because I felt so happy. I wasn't sure what this counselling was, but I liked the sound of it. Perhaps they were going to have another try.

I was also fantasising about Rosie, her sleek body, her beautiful boxer face and those long legs. I really liked Rosie in a respectful way. If dogs were to set up home together Rosie would be my first choice.

Humans got very hung up on us staying thoroughbreds, or else we became mongrels and I gathered that's not something to aspire to. If I were ever allowed to mate another dog it would have to be a black Labrador like me. Well what if I never meet a black lab that I love like Rosie – what do I do then?

I quite liked Tia but I dream about Rosie and I would like to have puppies with her. Who cares what they look like – we'd love them all the same? And we'd never leave our puppies because we'd just live happily. I am a really easy going dog and Rosie is beautiful so

Brown Eyes

it would be perfect. I have no idea how I'm ever going to wangle it though.

Once home, I sat waiting for my food, the highlight of most days. I scoffed it down pretty quickly, and took to my basket. I closed my eyes and drifted off and if I could smile I would because I felt so contented at the way things were going.

I was woken by a knock on the door. I didn't know how anyone had got there without my noticing, but I looked out of the glass bit where the cat comes in, and I recognised the feet. It was Phil. I leapt up and wagged my tail and started making whining noises.

'Hello Benji,' he was saying on the other side of the door. Hurry up Meriel, let him in. I was beside myself – I couldn't have wanted to see anyone more than Phil.

He looked funny and nervous though. And so did Meriel. What was going on?

He walked through to the kitchen, and she quickly ruffled her hair – women did that when they wanted to look attractive I think. That's good if she wants to look attractive for him.

'Thanks for coming.'
'What is it? Is it urgent?'
'Well in some ways it is.'
'Oh.'

Brown Eyes

He looked really miserable. What was going on here? I stopped sniffing Phil and decided to lie down and pretend I wasn't very interested.

Meriel made them both a cup of hot something and sat down.

'Elly's not been doing so well at school.'

'What you mean she's not top of the class anymore?'

'Well no. That doesn't matter, being top of the class, but it's why she's not doing well that's so important.'

'I suppose that's obvious in a way, isn't it? Is this what you wanted to talk about?'

He looked a bit irritated as if he didn't think Elly's A grades were important enough.

'No.' She sighed. 'I feel a bit nervous about this, but...'

'Yes?' he looked uneasy. What was going on?

'Well it sort of affects the children. I feel that we are mucking up their lives.'

'Like all the other kids they know – it's normal nowadays.'

'That doesn't make it right or easy.'

'No, I'm sure it doesn't.'

'I suffered a lot from my dad leaving and I was eighteen.'

'Yes, I know. And you've never forgiven him, have you?'

He sounded a bit nasty when he said that.

Brown Eyes

'No, I haven't. Do you want Elly to feel like that about you?'

'Look Meriel, if this is going to be a session of bashing me up and telling me how guilty I should feel then I might as well go when I've had my coffee.'

This wasn't going well at all.

'I've been thinking. I think we should have another go, and I know you probably think this is an awful idea, but I'd like us to go and see someone, you know.'

She stopped and took a deep breath,

'Relate, we need to go and see someone at Relate.

'Relate, aren't they the marriage guidance people?'

'Yes, but they don't call it that anymore. And there's nothing wrong with it. I can assure you nearly all of our friends have been at some point or other. It's not such a stigma and I've been told that it really helps people and I just feel that we could try and if you prefer to be with Laura and if I, well if I find I can't …'

'What?'

'Well – it's trust. It's so difficult you know. I can't...'

'OK, OK I get the drift. You don't have to keep on justifying it. Funnily enough I've had a chat with a few people, and I've thought about it a bit and we don't have to

Brown Eyes

tell anyone, so I'll go. But I only want to try it once and see what it's like. I don't need to have someone just telling me what a shit I've been.'

'I don't think they do that. I'm sure they don't. I know lots of people who've been and they all said it was really good. Who suggested it to you?'

'A few people but funnily enough old Aunt Jemima. I was quite surprised.'

Meriel smiled knowingly.

'When then, and where?' he asked.

This all sounded incredibly positive. They were going to talk to these relations people, and it seemed that worked for humans who loved each other from what they said. So, my life might just go back to being perfect again. If it was me, I'd just lick and lick the other person and not discuss it all, but then dogs can't really discuss anything – we just know.

'I don't know. I'd have to ring up but if you're willing, when are you available? Apparently, there's a waiting list if you go in the evening or Saturdays but it's OK in the week. I'm sure I could try and get away as long as it's not a Wednesday or Thursday. It's better if the children are at school because we don't want to have to say what we're doing, you know, give them false hope, or something whether it's false or not.'

She was gabbling very fast and then said,

Brown Eyes

'OK. If you don't want to. If you change your mind.'

'Meriel. I've said yes. Let's leave it there.'

He stayed a bit longer and then he gave her a kiss on the cheek.

'I thought you were going to ask for a divorce.'

'Oh.'

She picked up the talking machine as soon as he'd driven off, and I knew exactly what she'd do next. She spoke to Tania with that loud thing on.

'He's agreed. Can you believe it?'

'I'm thrilled. And knowing as I do that you love him I hope it works out for you Meriel.'

Immediately after I wondered if Meriel gone mad. She was singing this song and looking all happy and then crying her eyes out and still singing, 'We were so happy together, aaah'. And then she held my head and said,

'Benji, all you need is love. It's so simple.'

If only it were. To me it all seemed so very complicated with these humans. What could be nicer than to settle down and share your basket with someone and have puppies together? Except in my case, they'd be taken away and given to other people so I wouldn't get to see my puppies again unless I was very lucky.

With humans they did see theirs all the time, in fact they lived with them, but they

Brown Eyes

didn't appreciate them. They seemed to choose to split up their families so that they didn't see quite so much of their children. It all seemed crazy to me – they just didn't seem to appreciate what they'd got.

I wouldn't want anyone to think that I was unhappy. Well I wasn't until all this started. You see it's different for a dog – we could be happy being close to humans and I think we could make them happy, but they seemed to need more. We didn't always need more.

20

Jane

I looked at the couple in front of me. The woman had shoulder-length brownish hair and she looked anxious, which came over as not being very friendly. The man was more personable, but also looked incredibly tense, but then couples did when they first came in. What was noticeable about him was his piercing blue eyes.

It was obviously an ordeal because they didn't know what to expect when they came to meet this strange woman who was going to talk to them about the most intimate things in their lives. You always wondered which one of them was the driving force in getting them here and more than anything, were you going to be able to help them?

Quite often, quite frankly, there was no hope for some couples because one of them at least had decided before they came that they no longer wanted the relationship.

Other times you could see that the couple loved each other, and they were fighting each other and in danger of losing everything. In that case I always wanted so much to help

Brown Eyes

them to save their relationship, but it could go either way. I needed to stay impartial but sometimes situations touched a nerve because I was only human too.

Once we'd got all the formalities out of the way I asked them why they were here today. They looked at each other tentatively and the woman whose name was Meriel said,

'We're not living together, and we have to decide if this is how it's going to stay or if there's any,' she hesitated, and looked at the man, 'any chance, any hope.'

Her exterior was still cold but by the way she hesitated I could tell she was vulnerable.

'So why have you split up?'

She looked at the man again, Phil. He spoke,

'It's my fault. I had an affair and that's what caused it really. I'm not very proud of it but it just, well you know how it is - these things just happen.'

'I understand Phil,' I said, 'But I want you to know that there is no blame in this room. We won't get anywhere if one partner is going to feel that they are to blame. There are always reasons for infidelity and that is what we need to explore. We're all human and we all make mistakes, but we have to get to the current situation. Are you still seeing the other woman?'

'Yes.'

Brown Eyes

Meriel looked very aggrieved when he said this. She stared at the floor.

'OK, so I do have to tell you this. When a third party is involved it's difficult for us to take the course of counselling. I need to know what your intention is with this woman really before we can continue. Because if you are in another relationship it's going to be very difficult to work with you both. Do you understand?'

'I guess I'm just seeing Laura, that's her name, because I'm well you know, I've lost my children and my family, and I get lonely.'

He turned to Meriel.

'We had split up but when I heard that you were seeing this other chap,' he looked at Meriel, 'I thought you didn't want to get back together again, and Laura and I drifted back together.'

The woman was looking very cross at this point.

'So are you saying that if you and Meriel were back together this relationship wouldn't be continuing?' I asked.

'Yes of course.'

'What do you want, Phil?'

'I want us to get back together. I've been asking Meriel for ages. I want to get my marriage back.'

Brown Eyes

'But it's hard for a wife to choose to get back with you when you are seeing someone else.'

'But I wouldn't be if she wanted me.'

'Phil, are you saying that you are hedging your bets?'

'If you put it like that, I suppose I am?'

'Hmm. I feel that unless you put this relationship behind you, you cannot even consider going ahead with Meriel here.'

'Yes, there is that, but she's seeing someone too.'

I turned to Meriel.

'Is this right, Meriel?'

'Well it is, but I don't see the man very often. And I have to say,' she looked at him with a look that could kill.

'I thought that Phil had finished with this, this girl – she is a girl.'

'OK. I understand, but let's talk about you. You are still seeing someone?'

She went very red and couldn't seem to answer at first.

'It's well, it just happened. And if he was seeing Laura, why shouldn't I see someone?'

'It's not up to me to judge what you do. All I need to know is whether the two of you want to commit to your relationship and that doesn't include third parties. We have to establish that or else we are all wasting each other's time, aren't we?'

Brown Eyes

'Yes,' Phil said.

I looked at Meriel.

'Yes. It's not a problem, I keep putting him off anyway. It was an initial attraction and I guess it was because, because of what Phil was doing, and this man he was so nice to me, and I was alone, lonely I guess.'

'I'm not here to judge you, Meriel. Of course what you are saying is perfectly natural, but I have to ask you both the question, are you prepared to give up your new partners in the interests of making this relationship work?'

She nodded vigorously and he said, 'Yes.'

'Sometimes it's better to give yourselves space and to be alone to know what you really want. And, if we are working together, we have to feel that there is room for this relationship to flourish, not complicated with other people.'

'That makes sense,' Meriel said.

'Yes, I agree,' Phil said.

'Good.'

Let me ask you in turn and each tell me your own version, 'How did you meet? And what attracted you to each other?'

'We knew each other for a while,' she said. 'Phil's friend was friendly with an old friend of mine, and he was sometimes there when I met up with them. On most occasions we were

Brown Eyes

with other partners, but there was a time when we were both alone at their house.

Phil was talking to me differently as if he was really interested in me. It certainly sparked my interest and I wondered what I could do about it.

'And then out of the blue he called me and asked me out. To be honest it then happened very quickly and took us both, well me, by surprise.'

She smiled for the first time since she'd come in. I looked at Phil.

'I didn't think it happened quickly. I had liked Meriel for a long time, but she always seemed to be with a boyfriend. I used to wonder how we could get together, and so I just took a risk and rang her. And thank goodness, it worked.'

He laughed, and they smiled at each other seeming animated and happy, so how did it come to this?

Phil said to Meriel,

'And do you remember that waiter, the one with the funny lisp?'

'Oh yes,' she started laughing. 'I really enjoyed that time.'

It was as if I wasn't there. This couple loved each other still, but I had to get on with what we were here for.

'Sorry to bring you back to reality. I can see something between you but again it's up

Brown Eyes

to both of you. Are you both willing to do some work and relinquish other relationships?'

He nodded. 'I am.'

She hesitated, 'If Phil is sure, I am too.'

They said goodbye and I could hear them chatting as they walked down the corridor. I had a better feeling than I often do about some of my clients.

21

Jane

'When I was eighteen, I got home from school one day and my mother looked terrible. She put her arms round me and I didn't know what was going on but she said,

'Your dad has left.'

'What? "He can't have", was all I could muster.

'I was very close to my dad and I couldn't believe he would just do this. He'd left a note and just gone, and do you know I didn't see him for six months? He rang me out of the blue and asked me to go and meet him. I didn't get any sense that he regretted it when we met up.

'And when I was young, he always used to say to Leonora and me (that's my sister), "We'll always be a family and I'll always be here" and then he just buggered off without a word.'

She was getting very het up and I handed her the tissues.

'Thanks,' she said and blew her nose. 'I couldn't believe the betrayal. How could the

Brown Eyes

dad I loved so much just go like that and off with another woman and forget all about us? After all we're his children.'

'And did you ever come to terms with this?'

'Well it's not cool is it to be mooning around after your dad when you're eighteen? No, I guess I just got on with life and tried to have boyfriends and got very involved with someone for a long time who was fantastic to me. But I couldn't trust him and then there was Richard.'

She glanced at Phil as if this was a bit awkward.

'Does Phil know about this?'

She looked at him a bit sheepishly,

'I think so, do you?'

'Yes, a bit. Not much.'

She was crying now,

'I loved Richard to death. I adored this man and I just felt we had the most wonderful relationship. I'm sorry Phil. This is in the past.'

Now it was Phil's turn to look at the floor.

'But I knew that all the girls fancied him, and he wasn't immune to that at all, but we just had this chemistry and we were in love, so I thought. But then I would find out all the time that he was being unfaithful, or was he being unfaithful to them with me?

Brown Eyes

'I got so confused about whether or not I was his girlfriend. I loved him too much really that it was almost not real, but I noticed girls in shops looking at him and I almost couldn't bear it.

'It certainly wasn't good for my self-esteem, yet I'm sure I was besotted with him because when it was good it made me feel on top of the world, as if all my problems had evaporated, after having lost my dad like I did.

'But it was a real roller coaster - it just went on all the time. Someone would tell me that he was seeing a girl I knew, or I'd hear the answerphone message from some girl and all the time he'd tell me that they weren't anyone special. And then I caught him one evening when he hadn't rung me. I went round and a girl I knew (her name was Vicky) and they were just going out and I blocked his driveway with my car so he couldn't go out.

'He was so embarrassed that I was pleased, almost ecstatic, and I'm not a vindictive person normally. But we had this, I don't like to say too much really with Phil here because I don't want to diminish our relationship – ours is, was, so much more real than this was. But if you are besotted with someone you feel like you're in love with them all the time, but really it's a fantasy.

'I felt so betrayed by him and yet I thought I loved him so much that I didn't stop seeing

Brown Eyes

him and well, I guess only women can know what I mean. This was almost normal among my friends at the time, but in the end, I gave up. It came to the final straw when he asked my best friend out and I decided that I'd never go near him again and I didn't.'

'But the hurt is still there.'

'Yes. The hurt is, but I know it was a lucky escape for me. I wouldn't have wanted that kind of relationship long term. It was too tense and unnerving. In fact, eventually it felt liberating not mooning over him.'

She wiped her eyes.

'How did it feel to hear that story, Phil?'

'Awful. I don't feel jealous. I feel sad and guilty because I did the same thing.'

'Meriel did you feel that, when Phil was unfaithful, was it betrayal again?'

'Well I hadn't associated all those things – my father, Richard and now Phil. But yes of course it's happening again, and I just can't stand it. Why does it always happen to me?'

If I thought she was cold, it was just an exterior. She was so vulnerable and hurt, and I wondered if that was why all this had happened.

'OK Phil. I'd like to talk to you. Why do you think the relationship with Laura started?'

'Well I was finding that Meriel was very distant, very cut off and quite angry with me. And I, well you know – I'm a man. There was

Brown Eyes

this girl in the office, and I can't deny she was affecting me and the more Meriel distanced herself from me – you know sexually as well as emotionally – the more I couldn't resist Laura.

'And one night we were in the pub with the others from work, and she was talking to me, and I just knew I was going to end up with her that evening.'

'And that's the evening we've heard about, when Meriel heard you on your mobile phone.'

'Yes.'

Now Meriel was looking at the floor.

'I'm aware this can be painful for you Meriel, but we have to get everything out in the open before we can move on and try to heal the rift between you. I believe that if you two have come here together you want to try to repair your marriage. Is that right?'

'I have only just realised how loving someone doesn't just go away when things go wrong,' Meriel said.

Then she stopped speaking and put her hand to her mouth. We waited.

'And my friend, a very dear friend, died recently and I knew that if anything happened to Phil, I'd be so devastated and it has been me who has not wanted the relationship to continue and I just wondered if it was because of my hurt pride, and really I don't know if my feelings have changed for him.'

Brown Eyes

She gabbled this out very quickly and was going very red in the face, her eyes full of tears.

'Do you love Phil?' I asked.

'I just don't know. There's so much hurt, but I think it's deep down here somewhere. I just can't get it out.'

'Do you love Meriel, Phil?'

'Yes, I do.'

'So I suggest to both of you that you close the other relationships you have now and come back and see me when you have. I don't want to cause more problems between you but if only one of you comes back then that's OK.

'We can't take this any further unless you are open and honest and you don't have someone else in your life.

'You can't commit to this relationship unless you are both free to do so. It doesn't work with two other people in the marriage.'

'Like Princess Diana,' Meriel said and smiled. She was quite pretty when she let go of that cold exterior.

He turned to her and brushed her hand, 'I'm not Prince Charles though.'

They both laughed and I knew there was something between this couple that could be salvaged.

22

Benji

I was having the time of my life running around the park chasing Rosie and other dogs too. There was Jasper the cocker spaniel who sometimes growls at me, Poppy, another boxer, a large Alsatian named Jerry who was good fun, and the best of all, Rosie.

I felt as if I didn't have a care in the world and had put all the domestic strife behind me for once. It was as if I wasn't having to cope with a break-up, but that life was back to normal. It was sunny and Meriel looked happy as I ran around with the other dogs.

And then I saw him. I've nothing against Amber, his golden retriever, but I can say that seeing Jack in the park that day completely spoilt my fun. All the carefree moments were gone as I remembered that potentially this was my new master and Phil could be forgotten about.

I gave Rosie a quick apologetic lick on the lips and ran up to Meriel. If he thought he could have her all to himself then he had another think coming. Amber sniffed around

Brown Eyes

me a bit and I was polite, but I was looking at Jack.

'That dog of yours has got it in for me hasn't he Meriel?' he said as he kissed her cheek and tried to take her hand. But I'm pleased to say she took it away again.

'What's so urgent darling?'

Darling, what, how dare he?

'You're not pregnant, are you?'

I spluttered and then tried to pretend it was a sneeze. I didn't know women of Meriel's age got pregnant – what was he talking about? They must have been mating. I couldn't bear to think about it.

'What, at my age?'

That was a relief.

'Well it happens – my sister had her fourth when she was forty-six.'

'Oh God. Well no, that's not it.'

I heaved a huge sigh of relief and even gave Amber a quick lick but I couldn't concentrate on her. I had to listen to what was so urgent.

'Let's walk over there, Jack. I'm afraid it's not such good news.'

'Yeah. Is it about Phil? Is he moving back in?'

I couldn't help it, but my ears completely pricked up as if someone had said, 'Walk' or 'Bone'. This sounded too good to be true.

'Well not exactly.'

Brown Eyes

Disappointment.

'We have decided that we are going to try, you know for the sake of the children.'

'Oh Meriel, that's no reason to stay together. You know it won't work.'

'Well I don't really know that, and I'd like to give it a try and the counsellor said,'

'The what?'

'The counsellor, the marriage guidance – you know Relate, that's what they call it these days.'

'It's all the bloody same. Some social worker poking their nose into your business and telling you what to do. I hope you didn't tell them what we'd been up to.'

'Well not exactly, but you came up.'

'You didn't bloody analyse me, did you?'

'Of course not – you only came up in relation to me. You see they won't see us if we're seeing other people.'

'So can you see me when you've finished going?'

'Well only if it doesn't work out.'

'Which it won't.'

How did he think he knew what was going to happen to her and what was it to do with him anyway? I hoped Meriel had begun to see what a creep this bloke was.

'I want to give it a fair go, Jack. I'm sorry. You knew it was too early for me, I just wasn't ready.'

Brown Eyes

'It didn't feel like that when we were you know, close. I've never known a woman like you.'

The look on her face made me think she was going to give in and go back to him.

'Yes. It's been terrific, but I've got so much to clear up. It wouldn't work between you and me unless I do this.'

'So what are you saying? That you're sorting out things with Phil so we can be together?'

This bloke must be completely stupid. Couldn't he understand what she's saying?

'No, I'm not really. I'm trying to see if Phil and I can be a couple again and a family with our kids, which is what they deserve. There is so much at stake. You know, you've been married.'

'But Meriel look what he did to you. You can't trust a man like that. He screwed around and right under your nose.'

'I don't call one woman screwing around really.'

'And how do you know there weren't more?'

At this stage I could have bared my teeth and flung him to the ground. He was really getting up my nose. My tail was completely rigid and a little growl was coming out.

'Stop it, Benj. Sorry I don't know what the matter is. He normally likes Amber.'

Brown Eyes

'That bloody dog has always had it in for me.'

'Don't be like that, he's not a bloody dog.'

'To me he is. Sorry. Anyway, as I was saying you can't trust a bloke who puts it about and you know that. If you stay with me, I'll never look at another woman. You're everything I've ever wanted, and I wouldn't look at anyone else because you're so beautiful in my eyes. I've never experienced anything like the chemistry between us. It's amazing and I'm not going to let you go easily.'

'Please Jack. This isn't easy.'

'Because deep down you know that I should be with you, don't you? You didn't fake it – tell me, go on tell me, how good it was.'

'It was great. But this is my husband we are talking about.'

'Pity he didn't remember that when he got into Laura's pants.'

'Jack. Please, please. I'm trying to work on this with Phil and see if there's a way forward because we love each other.'

'Do you? Be honest, Meriel. Do you love him?'

I could see this was really hard for Meriel and her face was crumpling up and she was going to cry, and I just thought I'd nip his leg for that. How dare he upset her like this? I

Brown Eyes

pushed him with my hindquarters and he tripped and I felt better.

He tried to kick me. Surely that was enough grounds to get rid of him forever. He's a dog beater, but Meriel didn't even mention it.

'Please Jack. There's a lot behind all this, I can't tell you all about it because quite honestly, it's between me and Phil, but I know you're hurt and I know I've let you down. But this is life and maybe I'm wrong for having got involved with you, but Phil is the father to my children. We have history together.'

'Before he decided to ruin it for you. You mark my words but remember, I'll be waiting for you and I'm sure he can't fulfil you like I can. You've led me on a lot Meriel, you know. You wanted me just as much as I wanted you. Remember the night in the hotel. Just think about it Meriel.'

And with that parting remark he walked off with Amber looking back at me slightly apologetically.

Meriel sat down on the bench, all crumpled up. She was moaning quietly to herself,

'Oh God, Oh God, this is awful. Oh I wish I hadn't, I don't know, what can you do? I feel so awful, I shouldn't have, and I've upset him so much. I hope Phil's done the same with Laura. It's all such a gamble, Benji.'

Brown Eyes

And I was soon to find out. Funnily enough they seemed to want me along as a chaperone in these situations.

This was a first for me and I must admit that I really liked Laura. She had long hair and big, big eyes that were so friendly and she had a large mouth that seemed to be smiling all the time. She was quite tall and had a way of swishing herself around as if she knew people were looking at her.

'I wanted to tell you something today, Laura,' Phil said. 'I've brought Benji so we can have a walk together.'

'Oh how lovely. Hello handsome.'

I was melting. She stroked me all the time and said,

'What a lovely shiny coat. Has someone polished you? And beautiful brown eyes. You're gorgeous.'

This was of course addressed to me, not Phil, and I rolled over and let her rub my tummy. She was gorgeous as well and I could feel myself falling for her, but I wasn't supposed to because I was Meriel's dog. I couldn't start liking the woman who took Phil away.

What I couldn't believe was that Phil started saying the same things to Laura that Meriel had said to Jack, and I sort of knew why, because there was some plan they had to get together again. This was a thrilling prospect, and I could even forego having a

Brown Eyes

tummy rub from Laura to get what I wanted, although unlike with Jack, I actually felt sad for her.

'I'm going to tell you this straight. You and me we're going to have to finish, because I'm trying to get my marriage back together again.'

Her beautiful face just changed from fun and lightness to absolute horror as if he'd told her he was a dog snatcher or something.

'But Phil after all we've built up together. I can't believe it; I was hoping we'd have children.'

She just burst into tears, and he put his arms round her and she sobbed and sobbed. I was sure he wouldn't leave her in this awful state, and do you know I didn't even want him to? But I wanted him to get back to Meriel, and now I was feeling awful and started whining. It was just terrible.

'But I love you Phil. I've never loved anyone before, and you are everything to me. I wouldn't have moved in with you if I'd thought it wasn't finished between you and Meriel.'

'I know, and I thought it was finished too, but you'll meet someone of your own age. You will I promise. You don't want an old chap like me with two teenage children.'

'But I doooooo,' she wailed, sounding a bit like I do when they leave me in the car.

Brown Eyes

'Oh what am I going to do? Please, please don't leave me Phil. I just don't know what to do.'

'Look I am so sorry Laura. I never meant to hurt you but for me this wasn't a serious thing.'

'Ohhhh,' she looked even more upset.

'I mean you're a lovely girl but I stand to lose everything, and I know what I said, but I realise how much my family mean to me. When you have kids, you'll realise what it's like and how you just want to be with them day in day out seeing them grow up and that you miss out completely if you're not there sharing their lives with them. And much as you mean to me, I just can't let them go like that. I have responsibilities. They are always going to come first, and that's just how it is.'

'And Meriel? Don't you have to care about her?'

'And I do. Laura, I still love her. I'm sorry.'

'But you love me.'

'I like you a lot but I've never said that I loved you.'

'But I love you and I thought it was mutual.'

'I'm very fond of you, you are a lovely girl and I've never been out with anyone who was so much fun as you before, but I still love my wife.'

Brown Eyes

'Promise me you'll keep seeing me for a while.'

'I can't.'

'Why? Why?'

'Are you moving back in then?'

'No but I do hope I might soon. 'We have to sort things out.'

'How?'

'We have our ways of doing that, but I can't tell you all about it.'

'Why not?'

'Because it's not, to be frank, any of your business. You can think I'm a bastard, if you like, but I know you'll meet someone much better than me and one day you'll have your own children and I'll probably be very jealous.'

'I'll have to leave work.'

'Why?'

'Because I can't bear to see you there anymore.'

'You will get over me Laura. I am sixteen years older than you. When you get to forty, I'll be almost sixty – do you really want to be with an old man?'

'I just feel a fool.'

'Why?'

'Because you left your wife for me and now you don't want me.'

'I didn't actually leave her for you.'

'You did.'

Brown Eyes

'I didn't.'

'What do you mean?'

'She told me to get out because she found out that we'd slept together.'

'How?'

'I don't want to say.'

'Please.'

'It's of no relevance now.'

'You duped me. You told me you left your wife for me.'

'I let you think that, but I didn't say that. I'm sorry Laura. I hate to hurt you but I've been married for twenty years and I need to try and save my marriage.'

She moved back from him and loosened her hair and looked so sad with big drops of water coming from her eyes. She pulled him towards her.

'Just once more, Phil. Come on.'

He held her and then he let her go, and said,

'No. I want to try and get my family back. I'm really sorry.'

She picked up her spotted bag and stopped speaking. I was in the back of the car and I couldn't see if she was still crying but I heard a sniffling sort of sound. At that moment I wanted to climb into the front and nuzzle her. I don't like seeing these human women crying.

Brown Eyes

Phil drove fast and I kept falling from one side of the boot to the other. We stopped outside a building. He opened the back windows so I could breathe and locked the car. They went into this place and left me in the car, worrying that they'd get back together. I really wanted her to be happy, but even more I wanted him to be with Meriel so we could go back to our lovely family life again.

After a short while she came outside with a suitcase and he was carrying some other bags.

'Are you sure you want to go there?'

'Yes I do. I want to see my mum. Please take me there.'

'I'll have to drop off Benji, but I can't be seen with you in the car.'

'Didn't stop you last time.'

'I have explained.'

'I'll park around the corner and walk Benji round and then I'll take you to Exeter. This isn't easy Laura, and I know I've hurt you. I've also hurt Meriel and quite frankly I feel such a shit, but this is how it is at present.'

He stopped the car in the little road near ours and walked round with me on the lead. I looked back at Laura sitting in the front seat of the car and I stopped for a moment.

She was the picture of sadness and I felt hurt for her and all the family who had suffered so much since Phil went off with her.

Brown Eyes

He really had a lot to answer for, but to me he was my master and I still cared about him.

23

Benji

There was definitely something different about Meriel which I was very pleased about, but I didn't know what it was. Us animals can tell you know – we can feel the energy of someone whether they're feeling happy or very depressed.

Now I didn't feel as if I had to keep thinking about her and behaving well so that she wouldn't cry. In fact, I forgot all about her in the morning because we went to one of my favourite parks in the town.

As normal I started running round in the clockwise direction, past all the flower beds where I nipped in to have a wee and so on. I love this park because it's full of smells from other dogs, cats and of course foxes and there's a big path all the way round where Meriel lets me run.

Anyway, we went to where all the dogs were playing which was terrific and Tia was there and I joined in with everyone, but there's this dog I don't like who keeps growling at me if I pay much attention to Tia. So, we had a bit of a fight – we didn't actually

Brown Eyes

bite each other but the hackles were up and he was growling at me, so I growled back.

When Meriel was deep in conversation about teenage boys I ran off to the other side of the park. I don't know why I did it, but I wanted to be alone and not be told what to do. I could hear her calling and most unlike me I ran in the opposite direction. Finally, she saw me, and she was calling 'Benji' in this really cross voice. I'm pleased that she's not crying but I don't want her being cross all the time.

So I pretended that I couldn't see her and ran off even more. She was furious particularly as we were getting to a road, and I wasn't familiar with it.

Then she put me on the lead – you know how it is if you're sniffing something and you really want to carry on, they make you leave. I had the humiliation of walking past that angry male dog with the lead on, who just smirked at me and ran around even more.

When I got back to the car a woman came along with a huge dog, so huge it could have been a horse. And Meriel said,

'He's behaving really badly today. He kept running off when I got there.'

'How old is he?'

'He's five now.'

'Adolescent you see – he's behaving like a teenager.'

Brown Eyes

Meriel threw up her hands and said, 'Oh no I've got those at home, I hardly want another one!'

They both laughed hysterically. Very funny. If they could have seen underneath my black coat I was really blushing. I looked the other way. It was such a cheek comparing me to Rick who was quite badly behaved these days, while I'm always loving and kind. But and it was a big 'but', my lovely Meriel was laughing. After that incident and laughing at me, I didn't feel that friendly towards Meriel. I was sitting in her car because I wouldn't get out and go in the house, but then I saw Phil arrive and I got so excited I forgot all about it. Why was he coming round?

He went to the door and Meriel was laughing and smiling at him. Most unusual. And then she came to the car and said,

'I think he's sulking. He really misbehaved this morning, and I was furious.'

She handed him my lead.

Oh goody. Phil was going to take me for a walk, or better still they might come together. Just as I thought this, he said,

'Fancy a walk?'

'I'd like to, but I must go and pick up Elly – she's at Janey's.'

'OK.'

I didn't understand but we don't go to the beach anymore, and so I forgot about it and

Brown Eyes

then we went again. I just love it. I love the feel of the water on my body, and I like to shake myself vigorously when I come out. If I am too near to a human they scream and shout. Swimming is wonderful and who knew that dogs like me could do it?

There were often other dogs to play with and when it's not cold I can swim. I feel so free and excited when I swim. If it's very cold, I run around without getting really wet. Anyway, it didn't seem that Phil was going to take me to the beach today and we walked around to the park yet again.

I wasn't going to misbehave with Phil because I wanted him to see me as a model dog and want to come back and live with me. We were walking along the side of the river and then we came to the open area where they play with a big ball, and suddenly I saw the dog.

I don't mind her but it's her owner I was bothered about. Jack looked over and recognised me and walked over towards us. I was feeling awkward because he probably thought that Meriel was with me but when he realised, he'd go away. He kept walking towards us.

For once he said, 'Hello Benji,' as if he liked me. Normally, he was so irritated by me that he couldn't be bothered with me at all.

He came up and started stroking me and Amber was sniffing me at my rear end too. All

Brown Eyes

this attention and I didn't want any of it. Phil was looking and I wondered if he knew who this was. I went round the back of Phil with my tail down, my hackles on end. I wanted to show Phil that I didn't like this bloke.

'They often play together these two,' Jack said.

'Do they?' Phil answered but not in a friendly way.

'Well I've got quite close to Meriel.'

Phil just stood and looked at him as if he didn't understand.

'In fact I'm very fond of her and I don't want anyone getting in the way really.'

'Excuse me. Are you talking about my wife?'

'I'm sorry, mate. You gave up any thoughts of 'er being your wife when you went off with that tart.'

'Look I'm sorry. I don't know you. I certainly didn't invite this, and it's really got nothing to do with you.'

'You think it hasn't, but it has, because I want to offer Meriel a better life. I wouldn't run off with girls young enough to be my daughter and I really care about her.'

'So do I.'

Amber kept running up to me and bounding off, but I wasn't at all interested. My ears were right back now because of the fear I felt. I could sense strong stuff coming

Brown Eyes

from both of them. I was riveted to the spot because I was so concerned that someone was going to get hurt and I had to defend Phil. Besides, the idea of getting that Jack by the scruff of the neck was quite appealing.

'You should have thought of that before.'

'When I need lessons from someone else about my marriage, I'll ask thanks.'

'Look, while you've been running around at discos or whatever it is you do with young girls, I have been keeping Meriel company. We have got on extremely well, so well that I can't imagine her wanting you back again.'

Phil's eyes opened wide and then his mouth, and he went from pink to red and I thought he might explode.

'Please, Jack, is it Jack? This isn't necessary. What's been going on between you and my wife is to do with you both. But we have children and a family to think about, so I am sorry, but we are not divorced. You knew she was married.'

'What I knew was that her husband had done the dirty on her, that she was devastated and in need of tender loving care and I gave it to her. You mark my words it won't work out because she's too keen on me now and I'm not going to tell you how I know.'

'Good.'

'What?'

'Goodbye.'

Brown Eyes

I was sitting down by this time to stop Amber sniffing at me and because I was concentrating on what was going on. Jack was upsetting Phil.

Phil put me on the lead and walked off vigorously. Jack just stood there staring after us and Amber's tail was still wagging. What a stupid bitch, couldn't she see that this was hardly good fun?

When we got back to where we live, Meriel was drawing up in the car with Elly.

'Dad,' she yelled and jumped out and ran over and cuddled him.

'Hello darling,' he said. 'I've missed you.'

'Well,' he said to Meriel.

'Well, what?'

'Nothing.'

'Do you want a cup of tea Phil?' Meriel asked him nicely.

'I would have liked to, but I need to go. I've got a bit of a problem at work, and I need to go and sort it out. Knew it was too good to be true that I would get some time off this afternoon.'

His face was still red from his altercation with Jack. Was he going to tell Meriel?

'Are you alright?' Meriel asked. 'You look a bit strange.'

'Just harassed about this – well it's to do with a large order going through.'

Brown Eyes

'Oh.' Meriel looked bored and Elly had gone in to open a parcel that had come for her.

'OK. See you Monday then.'

'Yep. Bye Benji.'

24

Meriel

'I finished with Jack and it was awful. He said all this stuff about me never being happy with Phil.'

'Well he would, wouldn't he?'

'I suppose so. I think I've hurt him, but he took it very badly.'

'That's life Meriel,' Tania said gently. 'We all hurt people. You can't just do everything other people want of you.'

'No but the worry is I have difficulties trusting in this. Has Phil finished with Laura? He came over to take Benji for a walk and was very friendly, asked me to go with him which I couldn't, but when he came back, he was really odd.'

'How so?'

'He was all red in the face and when I asked him in for a cup of tea he said he had hassle at work. Tania, quite frankly I didn't believe him. I just thought it was Laura again. Perhaps he's having trouble with her, or has he even told her?'

Brown Eyes

'How will you know? When's the next session?'

'Next Monday. I don't know. He's capable of lying and then what's the point? You know I hate to even think this, but I think she was living there, in the flat he was renting.'

'How, how do you know?'

'The kids. He always takes them out and hardly has them round there. And when they have been round, she was there. Can you imagine? She's only a kid – he could have a daughter of her age.'

'Mm. I wouldn't focus on that now. All you can do is hope that he wants what you want, and quite honestly if he doesn't then you'll have to tell him to f… off.'

'Easier said than done. And I have blown it with Jack.'

'Meriel. You don't need a man all the time. If you've blown it with Jack then so be it, you'll meet someone else. But it is good to be on your own a bit.'

'Scary.'

'Maybe, but liberating too. I wouldn't ever want a man living here all the time!'

'Just one in your bed every now and then,' Meriel laughed. 'Only joking.'

'Well it's true. If you can find someone as sexy as Paul and you don't have to put up with them day in day out, then great!'

'I'm pleased for you.'

Brown Eyes

'It suits me Meriel. It suits me.'

'It's cold for the time of year, isn't it?'

'Have we changed the subject? I'd better go now. I'll pop in later as I'm going past.'

Tania burst back into our house a couple of hours later, looking as sexy as ever. She had a low bright purple top on, and her hair was gelled up at the front as if she were a young teen, but she looked great. Heaps of sex was doing her the world of good.

'What about Dave though? You must feel a bit sorry for him.'

'I don't. He wouldn't give a damn.'

'I'm sure he would. No man likes to think that his wife is off with a younger model.'

'Well I doubt it honestly. He wouldn't notice if he caught us at it quite frankly. He's always been in a world of his own and I am almost certain that it has included other women.'

'How do you know?'

'I've found evidence.'

'What kind?'

'Phone numbers, lipstick smears, and even a packet of condoms. Well he hasn't needed those for me for a long time!'

'I suppose looking at it like that, I'm amazed you've not said any of this before.'

'So am I. I think I've been the little woman who tried to suppress it. It used to upset me, but you know in recent years I've realised I

Brown Eyes

don't even like him. I don't like anything about him really, and as he gets older, he becomes grumpier and more unreasonable. And when he's had a drink, he's positively awful. So, if anyone else wants him they can have him.'

'So you will split up?'

'Undoubtedly. Changing the subject, I've got really back into yoga with Paul.'

I guffawed.

'What the tantric kind?'

'No, he's just reintroduced me to it and I'm finding that it helps me stay immensely calm and focused. I just love it. Why don't you try it too?'

'I could do with something to stop me yelling at the children.'

'Have you heard from Jack again?'

'He's a complete pain now. He bombards me with texts, and he's become quite wet about it all. I can't imagine what I saw in him, so instead of feeling kind and sympathetic I feel completely irritated by him. And then, when I've left him, I feel guilty. All these emotions, they drive me nuts.

'Yet, even when I was seeing him properly, he would say things like, "I don't know if you're as keen on me as I am on you." Or "Do you miss me when you're not with me?"'

'Heavy stuff. Too much in the early days when you've just split up with your husband.'

Brown Eyes

'Absolutely. How about Paul?'

'He's just fantastic. He's taught me things I didn't know even existed.'

'Oh wow, not *50 Shades of whatever*, is it?'

'No comment! I've never felt like this before and I feel as if I'd not lived until I met him.'

'This is real love then, huh?'

'Not really – real lust, I think. But obviously I'm not with him day in day out.'

'That's what kills relationships doesn't it?'

'What is it with men and flowers?' Tania added. 'When they're in a long-term relationship they can't be bothered, but when they're after you they shower you with them. Dave always said he couldn't understand why I liked them, but I do.'

'And that's what matters.'

'Yes, that's it. You think to yourself – if it takes so little to please a woman by buying her flowers, why not do it?'

'I just think men and women are so incredibly different that it's difficult to ever expect that you're going to be or feel the same. And the trouble is when you're young and in love you both compromise so much, but when the chips are down, and you're married it ain't like that anymore!

'I want to change the subject for a moment, Tania. I keep dreaming about Cathy and I miss her so much. I feel as if I'm overlooking her because of my other problems, so much that I feel guilty.'

'It's tough. I think about her all the time and wish it could have been different.'

Benji

I saw the flowers before Meriel did and I was thinking that she had been so wrong. I thought they were from Phil, and I was quite chuffed.

'Oh no Benji. He's not going to give up, is he?'

She thought they were from Jack, and she wasn't pleased. I wanted to growl just at the thought of him. I was going through all these emotions. If he was too nice to her, she might have him back and what about Phil? But hopefully, perhaps it would annoy her.

She just kept saying,

'Oh God, oh God,' and I didn't know what she meant.

She picked up the bouquet and smiled. Whoever it was, it made her smile.

She found a small envelope on the side of the flowers, and she picked it up and looked at it. I hoped she'd read it out. She opened the envelope and started to cry. No wonder men didn't buy flowers if they made women cry.

Brown Eyes

'Oh, oh,' she was almost wailing. This wasn't pleasant at all. She picked up the talking machine and punched at it with her fingers. As if they hadn't spent enough time talking to each other on that thing earlier, and when Tania came round to the house. She could be annoying.

'Tania, can you believe it? After our conversation, I have just got home and there's this bunch – no a bouquet - of the most beautiful flowers outside the door.

'No, I thought it was him and I was really bothered but, it's Phil.'

My tail involuntarily wagged itself and started banging on the fridge door making a lot of noise.

'Even Benji's excited. He's wagging his tail. I'm overwhelmed – the note, the note inside. Shall I tell you what it says? Yes, all right Tania, I will.

"I love you now and always will my darling – love and kisses, Phil".'

She was crying again. I just didn't know what's going on. One minute she was thrilled, the next she was crying. No wonder men got so confused about women, I am with them.

'I know,' she was sniffing and blowing her nose and talking at the same time. 'I'm almost scared that it could be good. It's never been good, and I don't know what it's like and this is so. I mean what shall I do? OK I'll ring him now. Let me go now and I'll do it straightaway.'

She put down the talking machine and looked in the mirror as if preparing herself to see someone but then she picked it up again. No one was going to see her so why did she scrape her hair with that implement?

She took a big deep breath and then I heard words I didn't think I'd ever hear.

'Hello Phil. These flowers are fantastic but most of all the card, it's what you said, and I must tell you know I love you too. Yes.'

She started to cry again. This was all getting too much so I walked out into the garden, but I couldn't help looking back at her to see if she was still tearful. She was wiping her nose but smiling and when she finished the conversation she yelled, 'Whoopee' and rushed upstairs.

Women!

Meriel

I started singing one of those sad songs that make you cry, even when you're not emotional.

And then I bawled my eyes out. What was the matter with me these days? Couldn't I get a grip at all? I turned round and Benji was just staring at me as if he was completely bemused. Well, so am I.

25

Jane

It's hard to tell when they walk in the room if any kind of shift has taken place amongst a couple and these ones aren't living together so it may be slower.

'Hello Meriel, and Phil, how are you both?' I looked at them individually.

He seemed to have a laid-back look which I couldn't work out. Maybe it was arrogance, maybe it was a defence from this whole process or maybe he didn't have the commitment that was needed. She looked anxious again.

'Yes, good,' he said.

'OK I suppose,' Meriel answered.

'I suppose?'

'Yes. I feel good at times and at other times I am petrified.'

'Can you say what you are petrified of?'

'All of this? I am so scared it's all going to go wrong and it's such a flimsy piece of thread that's keeping us together and I just don't know what's going to happen.'

'I see. Thank you. What do you feel Phil?'

Brown Eyes

'OK really. I just feel we have to wait and see but I'm very willing to make it work if we can do that here.'

'Do you think that you can do it here?'

'I don't know. I have my reservations.'

'Would you like to expand?'

'Yes. To be honest I'm not a great talker about this kind of thing and I'm not sure it's not better just to get on with it and not to analyse everything.'

'Do you find that difficult?'

'Not difficult. Just not necessary. Surely Meriel and I are intelligent enough to be able to work out our problems without having someone else involved. I don't mean to be rude.'

'No that's fine. I want you to say this. If either of you has any problems with the counselling, you do need to say so.'

'How do you feel about what Phil has said Meriel?'

'A bit fed up really. This seems to be typical of his attitude and dare I say it, this seems to be part of the problem. It's as if he can't be bothered and quite honestly, I feel like giving up now.'

'Yes, I understand. Do you feel that the counselling is helpful?'

'Yes, I do. Because I feel that things can't be sorted out between couples. If they could do it alone, why would so many people

Brown Eyes

divorce? I never thought that we would be going down that route but if he doesn't want to give this a go, I can't see any alternative.'

I looked at Phil and he answered.

'I want our relationship back and I have said I'll do anything to get it back so if Meriel thinks this is the answer then maybe we should try. I just don't find it easy because I wasn't brought up to discuss things all the time and it doesn't seem natural.'

'Most people weren't brought up that way, but that doesn't necessarily seem to be a good thing, Phil. Communication is the most important part of any relationship and when it is lacking things often go wrong between people.'

I'd seen this sort of thing before many times – maybe they have a lot they haven't said yet. I could tell that Meriel felt that there was something wrong with Phil. She kept looking at him sideways, and then she said to me,

'Can I ask Phil something?'

'Yes sure, go ahead.'

'What's the matter with you?'

'She's, she's pregnant.'

This was a shock and I had to fight my immediate feelings and stay professional. Meriel opened her mouth and closed it again. Her eyes filled with tears and she shook her head incessantly. Then she covered her face with her hands.

'Are we talking about Laura, Phil?' I asked.

'Yes of course, Laura.'

He sounded irritated.

'OK. So, what does this mean?'

'I don't know.'

'Do you think you should stay with her?'

'No, I don't want to. I don't know what to do. I'm so sorry, Meriel.'

'You should have thought of that before. Here we are having some farce of counselling and all the time you're getting her pregnant. What sort of person are you?'

'I know it sounds lame, but I haven't been seeing Laura. This happened before we came here, before we agreed. I can't believe it. But I'm not sure Laura really wants to be with me anymore, and of course I want to be with you Meriel.'

Meriel

I left that evening feeling heartbroken. It had all been going so well, but now this.

Tania called.

'What's up? I can tell something's wrong. It's in your voice.'

'Oh Christ. She's pregnant.'

'Laura?'

Brown Eyes

'Yes, fucking Laura.'

'Oh God.'

'Jesus Christ, the bastard.'

'But Meriel what's the difference? You knew he was sleeping with her, and you were forgiving him for that, and now she's pregnant. He didn't do anything different, it's just that she's pregnant.'

'What's the difference?' I almost yelled. 'Just that she's pregnant. He's having a baby with another woman.'

I was biting my lip, my voice wasn't mine, and I was going to burst.

'I think it's a pretty big deal.'

'But maybe, maybe you'll get used to it. He doesn't want to be with her, does he?'

'He says he doesn't and apparently she doesn't want to be with him. She says she doesn't want someone around who is more involved with their wife and family.'

'Sensible girl.'

'Yeah, I suppose so.'

'It's hard for you to see it but in some ways she's the victim here and if she's making a positive choice to not be with him, instead of pulling at him emotionally, that's good.'

'You're probably right. It's just – what does everyone say? What would the children feel? Oh yes, that's my brother or sister when my dad decided to go off with his other woman, or girl? It's so awful, so embarrassing.'

Brown Eyes

'Is that what you're really worried about Meriel?'

'Well yes. Isn't that awful? I'm worried about what other people will think. That's stupid, isn't it?'

'Not stupid. Pretty natural but let's face it at the end of the day it's how you carry it off. If you are happy with the situation, it will be OK. And don't forget this is another human being. One day when Joey or Jessy….'

'Hell, I hope they don't have names like that!'

'One day when they are grown-ups, you'll just accept it.'

'We've a long way to go before then and we have to tell our children if we're going to make a go of it. And it's a big ask.'

'Yup. They'll be OK. Children are very resilient.'

'I hope so.'

I hadn't been to yoga for years but this class was doing me a power of good. It wasn't just the exercise or the meditation, it was the person who was running it. She brought a special energy to the sessions, and I felt that I just wanted to be in the session all the time to soak it up.

I didn't speak to her about specific things in my life, but every week Babs would put up a little saying and they were just right for me.

Brown Eyes

One week it was, 'Live the change you want to see in the world,' by Mahatma Gandhi.

And that night I had a dream. It was one of those weird dreams that seem to send messages to you. I was on the beach and all around me there were people in their families, and I kept looking around, but I couldn't see anyone I knew. Then I saw Phil sailing past on a boat waving, and he went out to sea, and then I couldn't see the boat anymore and I was so distressed. I started wading in to see if I could see him. I wanted him to come back and he didn't, and I woke up and I thought I love him and that's it. If I love him, I don't want to let him go.

From that day on I felt there was just the possibility that I had it in me to make everything OK. If I could clear away all this festering resentment and the hurt, I could just accept Laura's child, who after all had not done anything wrong, apart from going off with a married man, of course. And if I could lead the way, everyone else – the children and even my mother – could accept the child too.

It was literally that simple. 'We make our own reality,' was another one of Babs' sayings. How true it was. Another one she'd read out was, 'The mind can make a hell out of heaven or a heaven out of hell. You choose'.

I wondered if I could just decide to choose. Why did I want to make a difficult situation more difficult? I had at last become convinced

Brown Eyes

that Phil was not interested in Laura, that he'd moved on and that the whole affair had been symptomatic of our own relationship being in trouble. And Laura had not only accepted that she didn't want Phil she apparently had a new boyfriend. He was in fact a former boyfriend, more of her own age and he cared enough about her that he was willing to take on the baby. Apparently, he'd never got over her and was very keen to get back with her.

The next big hurdle was to tell the children, and the one after that was to meet Laura.

I walked up to Jemima's flat which was in a beautiful Georgian house not far from the café in town. The sunlight was pouring in the window, and I sat back on the sofa feeling relaxed while we chatted.

She was nothing like my mum, she just wasn't judgemental at all. I told her all about Phil and Laura and the baby, and Jack.

I confided,

'Sometimes I feel that I can do this, but then I go through days of thinking it's completely impossible. It will never work and no one will be able to cope with it. Then I have other days where I think, of course we can make it work as long as we love each other enough, and I believe we do. We have so much history together and the love hasn't

Brown Eyes

really gone. But we've also got to get the children to accept it, which is hard.'

'The way you tell the children, if you are positive, is the way that they will receive it,' Jemima told me. 'You and Phil set the tone, and as long as you both mean it, they will accept it and just get on with their lives. In the future it will seem like a small amount of time in their lives.'

'You've been a great friend to me Jemima. You're very wise. I wish I could say the same about my mother. Thank you.'

'Well, Meriel, I have lived you know. I've had a fair few experiences of my own in my very long life. Come on, I've made us some soup and a salad. Let's sit at the table. Would you like a glass of wine?'

26

Meriel

It was now out of season and I could take Benji to the beach. They don't allow dogs on the beach between May and October which is understandable. He just loved it there and after a long warmish summer the water was still warm enough for him to swim. I stood watching him while standing in the shallows, with gentle waves lapping up to my bare feet.

There were lots of kite surfers around the estuary flying down like bats. This was obviously intriguing Benji and he wanted to go near, until one swooped near him. He quickly ran back towards me with his ears flopping up and down. We walked along the beach and up to the cliffs. The day was clear, and I stood looking out to sea feeling more peaceful than I had in a long while.

Feeling at peace was a rare and maybe a never-before experienced sentiment for me. The sun was out and the beach was quite quiet, so I had a strong sense of nature, with my trusty companion at my side.

We were slightly in limbo at the moment as I hadn't yet said that I could cope with the

Brown Eyes

Laura situation and we were no longer seeing Jane, because of this. However, I was talking to Phil a lot, and my gut instinct was that he was genuinely committed to us. In fact, I felt that he was so keen to get back together that he would do anything.

Laura appeared to accept it and had her new/old boyfriend, who sounded like a saint. To be honest, I think Laura realised that Phil was rather old for her. He said something that indicated this, but he didn't spell it out.

Funnily enough, when Phil and I met, mainly at home, we didn't talk about it, which is a bit weird, but sometimes you need a break. The kids loved him coming round and staying for dinner, but they must have been wondering why he hadn't moved back in.

Jack hadn't stopped sending me long messages and when he'd had a couple of drinks, he rang me and pleaded with me to take him back. That didn't make me feel good. I felt so guilty, but on the other hand I saw this behaviour as rather pathetic and wondered how I could ever have continued a relationship with someone who was capable of behaving like this. I felt that I'd have had more respect for him if he could just accept it like a man and not keep imploring me. If I didn't want to be with him, he can hardly have persuaded me.

Sometimes Phil and I went for walks together down at the beach and talked,

Brown Eyes

allowing ourselves to get to know each other maybe better than we ever did. We gave each other the time and space to talk. I wanted to get closer to him and hug him, but all we did was a polite kiss on the cheek as if we were just friends. We often stopped for a drink at the little café close to the beach, when it isn't raining. It just felt better being out with him and chatting than it ever used to.

It helped me so much to learn to relax more and try to be a bit more philosophical, not my usual frantic self who catastrophised everything.

As Benji and I were down at the seafront, he raced in and out of the sea, shook himself down and completely covered me in sand and water. Thanks a lot.

I thought I'd make this a long walk and start my regime of taking off a few pounds. We walked towards the cliffs and up the steep path. He was running ahead sniffing along the way and we went up past the golf club looking out to the blue sea with white sailing boats bobbing past. It was such a clear day that I could see the island in detail.

As we walked over the cliffs we dropped downwards, passing Thurlestone Beach and on to South Milton beach, where I sat outside the café, sipping a bottle of water before we carried on. Benji was on a long lead and started sniffing under the table, looking for stray chips and other bits of food as he always

Brown Eyes

did. Like all Labradors he was always looking for food.

I had to remember that we needed to come back as well, but I felt in the right mood for this walk so we passed the beach and went up the lane towards the cliffs which took us to Hope Cove. Up here there was still lots of purple heather all around and I was captivated by the azure blue of the sky with just a few clouds dotted along the horizon. It was so quiet and peaceful.

Once we'd got around the cliffs, I called Benji and we turned around to make the trip back to the car. And it struck me how nice it was not to keep worrying all the time, and just be able to enjoy what I'm doing.

I had butterflies in my stomach and kept thinking of ways to get out of it, but I had to meet Laura. It was as if in my mind she'd taken on the role of some kind of monster.

According to Phil, it was absolutely certain that she was happy with her current situation and her boyfriend was being very generous about it all. He must be a pretty amazing guy, or he just loved her a lot. But do people change that quickly?

One minute she was with my husband, the next she's having his baby, and suddenly it was all fine to go back to a previous boyfriend. A young man of her own age was obviously a better bet in the long run. It was hard to

Brown Eyes

imagine a young girl wanting a man in his late forties, but of course they often do.

I also gathered from Phil that Laura was pretty worried about seeing me. I think I'd have been more shocked if she wasn't. If she'd any decency at all, she perhaps ought to have felt guilty.

In fact, Tania had already said to me,

'She's the one who should be feeling bad after pinching your husband from you. I imagine she's pretty nervous.'

That was of course true, and it brought up some real pangs when I thought about it all. The strange thing was that because I had also had another relationship, I felt better. I think if I had been the victim wife with no other love interest, I would have found this impossible. But because I too had had a love interest, it made me feel confident. Was that weird?

When I spoke to Jane about it all she reassured me.

'No one wants to feel like the spurned wife, and somehow doing the same thing yourself doesn't mean it's revenge. It just makes you feel that he's not the only one who can find another lover. It's better for your self-esteem. I think it's completely normal.'

So the time had come. What to wear, not wanting to feel too frumpy as she was much younger than me. I made a special effort to look good as I didn't want to be outdone - in

Brown Eyes

truth. This meant trying on about three outfits before deciding on a long shirt, a big dangly necklace and matching earrings, and my black trousers. Due to all the upset I'd lost a stone, so I looked good in them, even if I thought so myself.

We arranged to meet in my favourite café in town outside in the garden. I took Benji with me, because he was back up for me. I parked in the harbour car park and walked across the road with Benji on the lead.

The nerves took hold of me as I was walking, and I didn't feel like myself. I walked round the back to the garden and arrived with about two minutes to spare.

The sun was shining in the garden of Courtyard Café as it always did and it gave me a sense of comfort, quelling the nerves. I saw her immediately – just as I had seen her before. Her brownish hair was back in a ponytail, and she looked incredibly young. She was reading a magazine and sitting at one of the big tables close to the flower bed. She glanced up. When she saw me she smiled and waved me over.

I was a bit taken aback that Benji looked so pleased to see her. He was dancing around, all excited but managed to have the decency to sit very close to me!

'Can I get you a drink?'

'No let me.'

Brown Eyes

'No,' I insisted. 'I'll walk up the steps and get them. Could you keep an eye on Benji?'

'Of course, could I have some green tea please?' Laura asked.

I climbed the outdoor steps and waited in the café. I bought a couple of brownies too and ordered a latte with soya milk. I took a few deep breaths to calm me down, but there was no real need.

When I got back, she said,

'He's been whining for you.'

'He can be a bit silly when I or any of the family leave him for a few minutes.'

'He's a lovely dog.'

Strangely enough, I liked Laura immediately. She came over as completely unthreatening, so I could feel the edgy nerves slowly melting away.

'I'm sure this is very difficult for you, Meriel and I appreciate you coming along to see me, but I guess if we are going to be able to deal with this situation it is the best thing we can do.'

It was hard to believe she was only twenty-five speaking to me with such a self-assured manner. I wish I'd been like that at that age, instead of being locked in insecurity. I looked at this girl (for that was what she was) that my husband had been so tempted by and I could understand why, despite myself. She was

Brown Eyes

warm and friendly and a man feeling unloved by his wife might well fall for her.

'Thanks Laura. It isn't easy but I believe we can make it better if we all try and get on. Obviously, your child needs to know his or her father.'

'Her.'

'You know already?'

'Yes. I went with my boyfriend yesterday and we saw a scan and it was amazing.'

'It is, isn't it?'

'Did they have scans when Ricky and Elly were born? Oh, sorry that sounds rude.'

She obviously knew their names.

'No, I know what you mean. But even back then they did, and I remember with Ricky, I couldn't believe it. The first and all that. Are you pleased it's going to be a girl?'

At the same time as I was speaking to Laura, it was running through my head,

'I am discussing my husband's future child with another woman. Life is completely crazy. Can I really do this?'

'Delighted and so is Jed,' she responded.

'He's your boyfriend.'

'Yes – he is really excited.'

'Isn't that fantastic? And he doesn't mind.'

'No, he just says he loves me so much and the baby will be ours. Well, you know. Obviously not just ours.'

Brown Eyes

She squirmed with embarrassment, and her cheeks flushed red.

'I think I understand. She will be living with you, but it will be nice if she is part of our family too.'

'That's incredible of you to say that. I didn't think you would.'

'And quite honestly she – I guess she doesn't have a name yet – didn't ask for it to be like this. She is perfectly innocent.'

I could barely believe I was saying all this. It was as if a much nicer person than me had taken over my voice. I have always been so stubborn, but it was only when Jane actually pointed that out, that I wondered what the advantage of being like that was? It didn't help anyone, and I was the only one stopping our family from getting back together again and making it work.

It wasn't all about me, and I had to consider the kids and Phil, and what they all wanted, but deep down it was what I wanted long-term too. Even when Laura had her daughter, we would still be a family.

'Oh yes. It's good of you to see me and not want to stick pins in me.'

'A lot of water has gone under the bridge, Laura. There are reasons for problems in marriage and I guess we've discovered ours. Without being rude, because I don't mean it that way, it was waiting to happen and you

Brown Eyes

came along. It could have been anybody, if you take that the right way.'

'Yes. You're probably right. I was vulnerable too and these things happen. And now I can't regret it because of my baby, but you know, life has its funny ways. In fact, I had split up with Jed when Phil and I, well you know. I guess I was feeling pretty sore about that, and now we're back together our relationship is better too, so I sort of know what you mean.'

I finished my coffee and started to gather up my things.

'I had better be going. Got to pick up Elly and a friend.'

'I guess I'll be doing that in a few years.'

'Let's hope that we can be supportive to each other because that's the only way forward.'

'Thanks, Meriel. I really appreciate it. I won't hide it, but I was worried about meeting you, and it's been really good.'

'Come on Benji.'

He jumped up and I said,

'Bye, nice to meet you,' and that was it.

Something strange was happening to me. My husband was about to be a father again with another woman which could have been a huge mess, but I felt joyful as if all the burdens of my entire life had been lifted. Who'd have believed it – certainly not me?

Brown Eyes

Benji

I was in seventh heaven. I had been to see Laura with Meriel. It was a bit obvious that I knew her already but instead of sitting with her and flirting, I had to make myself be loyal to Meriel. I just sat with her. This was very strange, but at last they were behaving like canines instead of silly humans. And I have to say I admired both of them for not having a fight or biting each other or anything.

And then something rather momentous happened and I had the best day of my life. It had nothing to do with the Stevensons at all – or at least they might have thought it was, but it was one of those dog things that happens, and humans are not a factor. I was on my way back from a walk with Meriel down by the water that goes to the sea. I was jogging along, minding my own business when this spaniel bitch who I'd met before suddenly appeared and was extremely pleased to see me. Fortunately, Meriel kept walking and wasn't paying much attention to me.

She smelt rather good, and she was coming on so strong to me that I got carried away, and quite honestly, I got lucky. I had never done this before, but it seemed quite easy particularly as the spaniel obviously knew what she was doing. Meriel, had walked past the fence and was nearly home. She kept

Brown Eyes

calling me, but I obviously wasn't going to go, and in fact by then I couldn't anyway.

So, Meriel walked up just as we were separating, and she looked very confused and asked what we were doing. Hadn't she learnt the facts of life? I hadn't done this before, but Tess (that's the bitch) showed me that you stand back-to-back until it's finally finished so we were sort of connected.

Meriel obviously didn't know much about this either because she kept instructing me to come home. As if I could. It was really embarrassing with her standing there patting me on the head and I was looking at her as if to say,

'Please go away, this is private.'

But it took her ages to cotton on and then she ran off to tell Tess's owner, who was walking along fast looking for her. It was rather awkward.

Then can you believe it she kept telling everybody, and I mean everybody? This was my private business and she thought she could tell everyone. For one moment I felt as if I knew why Phil had left her and then I felt guilty for being so mean, because I loved her really, but why did she have to go telling people?

Now, all I just wanted was to see Tess and experience it again, and they wouldn't let me go and see her. I got the impression I wasn't supposed to have done what I did but I don't

Brown Eyes

know why. It was completely normal and natural and I'm a bit fed up with being treated like a silly puppy. And it wasn't as if I went looking for her, she came and found me so I couldn't be blamed.

27

A year later

Meriel

Everything seemed so different now. Listening to my friends moaning about their husbands, I realised that it was a two-way thing. Women love to moan about men, but it's usually partly their fault. Everyone has their baggage and if they were never going to be introspective as well how could they make a success of a relationship?

'You know, Tania, it sounds crazy but I am so pleased that Phil had his affair with Laura.'

Tania's mouth dropped open. She thought for a few minutes and then said,

'Yes, I do know where you're coming from. You wouldn't be feeling so much happier if it hadn't been for her, would you?'

'No and we appreciate each other so much more. And would you believe it the kids just love little Emmy? She's a new dimension in their lives. Some people might say that it was appalling for them, so sad, and so destructive,

Brown Eyes

but actually it's that kind of thinking that does all the damage.

'Nothing is a problem if you're prepared to accept it. I've got a much nicer husband, a happier marriage, my children have another sibling and life at home for them is much better than it would have been if we'd carried on the same old way.

'And quite honestly I know why Phil went off. I was a starchy, screwed up, cold woman.'

'That's a bit harsh.'

'But true. I didn't know what I'd got. I just saw him as an ogre because he's a man, and it's so easy to do that when other women are doing it too. It's just fashionable to complain about your husband and as you know lots of people don't manage to make a go of a relationship.'

'Like me. I admire you, Meriel. You stuck at it; you did the hard bit which is that you changed yourself. And the fact that you went and met Laura. Wow, that takes some doing.'

'But it didn't. That's the point. Because my ego wasn't in the way and because I didn't feel so unloved anymore, I could just see Laura as the one who was the catalyst for my marriage to improve and who can blame her really? We can't all be high and mighty and think that we wouldn't do what she did under the circumstances.'

Brown Eyes

'Very benevolent of you, but I know what you mean. I've not been averse to the odd married man.'

'What recently?'

'Well, chance would be a fine thing!'

'No actually just before I got married. I had this really exciting fling with someone and quite honestly it was very exciting. There was so much passion. I used to work with him, and I knew he fancied me. He was a serial adulterer, but he had the gift of the gab and he kept asking me to work late. Well after I'd done it once I was always working late!'

'Tania. There's lots I don't know about you isn't there?'

'Probably. I've had a life you know!'

For once in my life when I set off to see Mum, I wasn't worried about what she was going to say. And this was something to do with my new-found confidence. Now I really knew what I wanted so I seemed to have become more sure of myself.

I kissed her on the cheek and she made me a cup of tea. She was looking remarkably sprightly for a seventy-five year old. She had a long red and orange Indian scarf wrapped around her neck, her hair had been coloured so there was no hint of grey, and she was looking slim and attractive.

'How are things?' she asked me.

Brown Eyes

'Good.'

'Have you patched it up with Phil?' She sounded genuinely interested with no hint of criticism or sarcasm.

'I think marriages go in cycles you know,' I told her. 'And it's how you get through the really bad bits and stop believing that he doesn't care and it's a waste of time. And having an affair is just a symptom of all that. But it's so easy to break up because both of you feel that the other one doesn't care, and I'm sure people get divorced and just persuade themselves they don't care.

'I don't want that to happen to us. We've had a major crisis, but we love each other and at the end of the day that's what matters.

'All of us feel insecure about love because hardly anyone grows up feeling truly lovable, so when things are going wrong it plays into this insecurity. We feel unloved and then resentful and that's when the trouble starts. Someone else comes along who makes us feel loved – for a while at least! This can't possibly apply to everyone because some people need to move on, but I bet there's a whole load of divorces that aren't necessary.'

Mum hadn't said a word, which was odd. I realised it was so unusual for me to talk like this at all, let alone to her. I peered into her face,

'Why aren't you saying anything?'

Brown Eyes

'I was just thinking Meriel. You've really grown up during this whole episode. And what you were saying was very wise. I was just listening.'

I felt completely stunned. Was this my mother? Things were really changing.

28

Benji

I did something today that I've spent my whole life trying to do. I caught a rabbit. I was so excited and so pleased. I knew that Meriel would be pleased with me, but she most certainly was not. She kept shouting and screaming so I hung on to the rabbit with my soft mouth and she kept saying, 'Drop it, drop it' so I did.

She wasn't horribly cross with me, as she's usually in a good mood these days. Life has changed so much for the better that I know that I'm a very lucky dog again.

At last, I could see that they were happy. I don't know what it was before, but it wasn't true happiness. Not that everything was wonderful all the time because life doesn't seem to be like that for humans or dogs, but there was a sense of calm and a feeling that there was love all around us.

Brown Eyes

Meriel

There was Phil in that awful brown jumper his mother had bought him fifteen years ago. He was manoeuvring the hose around the garden to wash his car obviously oblivious to the fact there was a hose pipe ban on at present. He always did this in the most peculiar way, weaving his way in and out of the garden chairs and past the gate so that the hose was entangled here and there along the way.

All those irritating things that he did but he is the man I love. If he wasn't here, I'd miss those habits like leaving empty coffee cups all over the house, forgetting to put his towel back in the bathroom, and leaving piles of socks behind the chair in the bedroom. What a joke!

His horrible jumper and even his unshaven stubble I would miss because it was the whole person, the sum of the parts who has shared my life for such a long time, whom I never wanted to lose. He might not be exciting, and he did find someone else for a while but he does love me and our children and what more could you ask for?

What's surprising to me, is that one of the best results of all of this turmoil and upset, is that I have changed. I knew I was stubborn – partly because my mum and Phil told me (a

Brown Eyes

lot), and I recognised it to be true. I could actually turn down something I wanted to do because I was being stubborn. Usually because someone had said the wrong thing to me, and I wasn't going to allow them to win. Where all this came from I don't really know, but I suppose it was from childhood and having such an awkward mother.

It's not as if I realised what I was doing, but I would feel so angry and then when I'd calmed down, I wondered why I hadn't just let myself do something that would be enjoyable. People are weird and I was one of them. Now, I can allow myself to enjoy life without having the compulsion to spoil it for myself and everyone else. The Laura situation was so huge that if I could accept that, I felt I could accept anything.

My life was so much better.

When I came close to losing you, I realised how much I cared
I can feel it in my heart and soul
Now I know what it feels like to lose you
I feel all this love for you that I didn't know was there.

OTHER BOOKS BY FRANCES IVE

FICTION

Finding Jo, a novel set in a retreat in the Himalayas, January 2021

NONFICTION

One Step Ahead of Osteoarthritis – tips to help people stay active and mobile
Give and Take with a Capital G & T – true stories from the 20th century about marriage

CAN YOU HELP?

Reviews are everything to an author, because they mean a book is given more visibility. If you enjoyed this book, please review it on your favourite book review sites and tell your friends about it. Thank you!